DIVIDED EMPIRE

VAL TAUBE

www.mascotbooks.com

Divided Empire

©2020 Val Taube. All Rights Reserved. No part of this publication may be reproduced, stored in a retrieval system or transmitted in any form by any means electronic, mechanical, or photocopying, recording or otherwise without the permission of the author.
The views and opinions expressed in this book are solely those of the author. These views and opinions do not necessarily represent those of the publisher or staff.

For more information, please contact:
Mascot Books
620 Herndon Parkway, Suite 320
Herndon, VA 20170
info@mascotbooks.com

Library of Congress Control Number: 2018911249

CPSIA Code: PRV0919A
ISBN-13: 978-1-68401-493-4

Printed in the United States

DIVIDED EMPIRE

Val Taube

CHAPTER 1

Washington

General John Peterson was awakened by a phone call.

"Get up," said a harsh voice on the other end of the line. "You're leaving in two hours to meet with the members of NATO."

"Brussels?" John mumbled.

"This meeting will be in Italy—Naples, actually. It's already 2:30. I haven't gone to bed yet and probably won't now. I'm sorry friend, but there will be a car outside your home at 4:30. Please pass on my apologies to Barbara for disturbing her peace."

John quietly slipped from bed, glancing over at his wife. He clutched the phone to his ear as he searched in the dark for his things. "And the purpose of this meeting?"

"The Ukrainian people intend to separate from Russia and join the European Union and NATO. Our intelligence reported that the Kremlin has moved their troops to borders of Ukraine. Sean will brief you on the way to the airport and give you the necessary documents."

John paused, contemplating the news. After a brief silence, the voice on the other end continued, not quite as harshly as before.

"Of course, by the time you arrive in Naples, some of the documents will have already become history. John, it is critical that this history be aimed in the right direction to prevent something terrible from happening. We're talking a third world war."

A black SUV with tinted windows pulled up to John's house at exactly 4:30. Two lights were on in the house, but they went out one after the other, plunging the house into total darkness. The front door opened, revealing a tall, strongly-built man dressed in a military uniform. The gray hair beneath his military peak cap and chest decorated with medals spoke to a life of doing and seeing difficult things. He gave off an air of athleticism and intelligence. In his left hand, he held a portfolio; in his right hand was a coffee mug, with a cloak slung over his arm.

On the way to the airport, Sean, a senior analyst from the US State Department, informed General Peterson about the ongoing situation between Moscow and Kiev. On Thursday, February 20, a bloody clash had erupted in Kiev, the capital of Ukraine, between the pro-Western Ukrainians and the special forces of President Yanukovych, Putin's protégé. Eyewitness accounts indicated that snipers were shooting at the demonstrators, aiming at their heads, necks, and chests. The medical services coordinator declared that more than a hundred people had been killed.

Sean explained that intelligence services had intercepted radio communications between the snipers and their coordinators. They spoke in Russian, without an accent. The order to shoot at the protestors—supporters of the European Union and NATO—had been given by the Ukrainian president and sanctioned by Moscow. Additional reports suggested that Yanukovych was trying to escape to Moscow through Crimea. The Ukrainian secret service had attempted to hold him in Yalta, but at the last moment someone warned Yanukovych and he changed his route to pass through Sevastopol instead. From there, he was delivered via a Russian landing craft to Novorossiysk to ask Putin to accept him in Moscow.

"What does he want from Putin?" General Peterson asked, interrupting Sean's briefing.

"Excuse me, sir. It is not what he wants from Putin, but what Putin wants from him—for him to stay in Ukraine. Yanukovych is Putin's only chance to keep Ukraine under his control and prevent it from joining the EU and NATO. Yanukovych's desertion of Ukraine also means Putin's hopes are jeopardized." Sean shuffled through his papers. "According to our intelligence data, we have every reason to believe that a full-scale Russian invasion of Ukraine is possible. If this happens, then further consequences may be unpredictable."

"What's the situation in Crimea?"

"Sir, we know that there are already a large number of *Spetsnaz* in Crimea. All of the Russian Special Forces are civilians who have entered the peninsula from all directions under various guises— tourists, workers, students, and so on. There are more and more of them with every hour."

"What do we know about Putin's tactics and strategies in Crimea?"

"Putin's headquarters is dealing with a bloody Chechen option that is playing out."

The General exhaled through clenched teeth. "So we must help our allies to do everything possible for Ukraine to not become a second Chechnya."

"Absolutely, sir."

John nodded and looked out the window. The sky was lightening, and he could see the floodlights of the airfield up ahead. *Is this all really happening again? It's as if Khrushchev has been raised from the dead,* he thought. As the SUV pulled up to the plane's ramp, Sean handed the general a folder full of documents. The words "Top Secret" were stamped across the top of the folder.

"Everything you need, sir. Only for your eyes. Have a good flight, sir."

The General placed the folder in his briefcase without opening it, opened the door, and walked to the Pentagon's passenger jet. The Captain stood at the ready and saluted John as he boarded, then ushered him into a private office with a soft leather sofa chair and desk.

"The blanket and pillows are here on top, over your head," the Captain said.

The General nodded, then asked for some strong coffee. "And another request," he said, "Please ask the attendant not to disturb me unless it's urgent."

The General put the briefcase on the table, took off his coat, and wearily sat down to wait for his coffee. The attendant brought the French roasted coffee and swiftly departed. General Peterson took several sips, then pushed the coffee mug aside, opened his briefcase, and pulled out the folder with the documents.

He spent the next ten hours reviewing the documents, transcripts of telephone calls, and personal notes. When the attendant knocked on the door to tell him they'd be landing soon, the General was startled. He had become so engrossed in the documents that he had almost forgotten that he was on a plane. He put the documents back in his briefcase, held his briefcase on his knees, and leaned back in the chair. He closed his eyes, but still could not fall asleep.

The times are different, but the problem is the same. After so many years, here we are again at the doorstep of a nuclear catastrophe.

As the plane started its descent into Italy, John fastened his seatbelt, wondering if he should even bother.

Naples

At exactly 9:45 PM, General Peterson's black Mercedes stopped near the main entrance into NATO. He had fifteen minutes until the meeting was set to begin.

He stepped out of the car into a warm Italian night. They were meeting in Lago Patria, a small town on the Mediterranean coast about 150 miles south of Rome. It was the home of NATO Allied Forces: a command center that managed, controlled, and protected the political, economic, and territorial interests of the allies. Their headquarters was also a masterpiece of modern architecture, a pinnacle of technological inventions.

The silver metal walls of the distinctively shaped building reflected the soft light of hundreds of fluorescent lamps. NATO member country flags proudly swayed in the fluorescent fog. A titanium blue light shone over the main entrance, adding a hint of mystery to the NATO emblem. Suddenly, a gust of wind brought one of the flags to life. Thirteen stripes flew up to the starry sky, and moonlight brought the fifty stars of the United States to life. John hurried inside, knowing the hope and support of many countries, and the dreams and aspirations of millions of people, depended on the decisions made in this building.

The conference room was equipped with the latest technology, and was quite comfortable. John could look at almost any point in the world without getting up from his chair thanks to the large, high-quality monitors along the walls. The advanced technical equipment allowed for the monitoring of multiple strategic targets of both NATO and its opponents. Such capabilities enabled the real-time coordination of NATO operations across the globe.

Nearly all of the NATO countries were represented. The room was extremely diverse, with military and other leaders from many different backgrounds. As usual with these meetings, a certain amount of tension hung in the air.

Once everyone was seated, the Commissioner for Eastern Europe, General Albert Friesen, started the conference. He provided an overview of the critical situation in Eastern Europe, underscoring the threat of the imminent full-scale war between Ukraine and Russia.

"If this war breaks out, then whether we want it or not, it will involve all of Western Europe," he said.

One by one, the attendees shared the information at their disposal. General Peterson was last to speak.

"First of all," he began, "on behalf of my country, I want to thank everyone present for their contributions to our common cause—the preservation of peace and democratic principles throughout the world. The United States government requested that this emergency conference be held for one main reason: We have specific and reliable data, as General Friesen has mentioned, concerning plans for a full-scale Russian invasion of Ukraine and Moldavia. Western Europe remains in question."

He paused to pull two magazines from his briefcase and place them on the table.

"Do these look familiar, gentlemen?"

The cover of a faded *Time* magazine showed a photograph of Adolf Hitler under the headline "Person of the Year." The more recent *Time* cover showed a photograph of Vladimir Putin with the same headline.

"Couldn't you find cleaner copies?" The French General Roland Martel fingered the tattered cover with Putin.

"They're from my personal collection." When no one else spoke, John shrugged and said, "I like to collect 'Person of the Year' memorabilia."

The English Admiral Robert Adams grabbed the magazine with Putin. He studied it closely for a moment before holding it at arm's length. He twisted his upper lip into a sarcastic smile. "I just don't understand it. Out of 140 million people, the Russians really could not find someone more intelligent for president?"

He tossed the magazine on the table. "Anybody else see the photograph of him sitting bare-chested on horseback? Like he was trying to play Rambo."

"Was he a good Rambo?" John asked.

Admiral Adams rolled his eyes. "Maybe a skeleton of Rambo." He snorted. "I heard a rumor that you once wanted to recruit him for the CIA. Any truth in that?"

This time it was John's turn to scoff, although more discretely than had Admiral Adams. "Hiring someone with his abilities would bankrupt the CIA. We don't accept people with his reputation. And if they mistakenly appear there, they don't last long." He picked up the two magazines and slid them back into his briefcase. "But today we are here for a different reason, gentlemen. We have learned that Russia's official invasion of Crimea is imminent. It's scheduled for March 1. Russia plans to retaliate to a so-called threat to the security of Russian citizens by Ukrainian nationalists called Banderas."

He looked around the table, but no one spoke. All eyes were on him, waiting for him to continue.

"During and after World War II, Banderas fought against the Soviets for the independence of Ukraine. They were never in Crimea. But now—if they are still alive—the youngest of them are probably more than eighty years old." He paused for several of the attendees to finish whispering to their neighbors. "I think it is clear to all of us what kind of 'threat' these few elderly men are to hundreds of thousands of Russians and their military."

General Friesen cleared his throat. "Doesn't Putin realize how much Crimea will cost him and the Russians?" Those around the table nodded in agreement. "Today they're shouting, 'Crimea is ours!'—completely forgetting that the money is ours. It's not in Russia where dollars grow."

John shook his head. "He's stuck in a dream of restoring the Russian empire. The people believe in his rhetoric—propaganda has become the norm." He glanced down at a summary document on top of his file. "His phrases like 'a threat to Russian citizens' or 'discrimination against Russians or the Russian-speaking population' have already been adopted at every level of his administration, both inside and outside the Kremlin. They never miss the chance to add the idea that 'Russia will protect them, the Russians, or the Russian-speaking, wherever they may be.' Such a potent idea as discrimination against Russians can be triggered in any corner of the world where there are Russian-speaking people, especially the former republics of the USSR." John looked around the table, meeting each person's eyes. "Putin's nostalgia for the former USSR, his empire ambitions, and his pathological narcissism are a serious threat to global security."

"So are we to gather all of these Russians and deport them to Russia?" Admiral Adams asked. "We've got more than enough of them in London. We warned you about Putin. Even some of our Russian oligarchs tried to stop his victory. Damn shame they were too late."

"Putin doesn't need the Russians in Russia," John replied. "He needs them where they are, where he can manipulate them to accomplish his political goals."

The room fell silent. Everyone imagined the kind of horrors Putin could perpetrate with his army of Russians scattered throughout the world, disguised as ordinary citizens. Several attendees shifted uncomfortably in their seats, their imaginations obviously showing them something they did not want to see.

"Yesterday, a former KGB employee who works for us now told me a joke." All heads turned to John, waiting. "One of Putin's oligarchs moved to Ukraine—Odessa, I think. After some time the Ukrainians asked him if he was worried about forgetting Russian, but the oligarch said he has no problem with Russian or Ukrainian. Then they asked him if he's afraid of the Banderas, and he answered that he had never seen them. Amazed, they asked him if he was afraid of anything, and he replied, 'I'm afraid that Putin will come to liberate me'."

A handful of chuckles scattered through the room.

"Make no mistake about it," John said, his voice hard and serious. "One wrong reaction to Putin's ambition and we will find ourselves on the threshold of a third world war. He has openly stated that he is not afraid to use tactical nuclear weapons in Ukraine. Russian TV channels constantly talk about turning the United States into radioactive ash—and we're talking about discourse that far exceeds the vulgarity of anything we encountered during the Cold War.

"The old Soviets have kept World War II fresh in their memories all this time. They still remember the smell of the gunpowder and feel the tanks rumbling through their towns as if it were yesterday. In my opinion, they know far too well how much worse a nuclear war would be."

"Explains why they were able to end the Cuban Missile Crisis in a peaceful manner," Admiral Adams said.

John sat back down, his briefing concluded. Next on the agenda was General Sanchez of Spain, slated to give a military overview of the evolving situation. Sanchez stood up, and pulled out a stack of papers from which to read.

"According to our intelligence data, Crimea already has rocket complexes with 'Bastion' coast protection and TU-22MZ strategic supersonic bombers. The combat radius of these bombers is approximately 2,400 kilometers. Their main armaments are the X-22 and X-15 cruise rockets, which could bear a thermonuclear charge. The range of their flight is 250 to 500 kilometers at a speed of 4,000 to 6,000 kilometers per hour. Russia plans to deploy modernized TU-22M3M bombers to Crimea with new X-32 rockets by 2020. The range of these rockets will be up to 1,000 kilometers."

General Sanchez looked up from the document. "In other words, not only Turkey, but also Western Europe—including Great Britain—will become possible targets not only for Russian ballistic rockets, but also for strategic Russian aviation."

"Are you prepared to act if Putin violates your territorial space?" General Martel asked.

General Sanchez waved a dismissive hand. "If one of these strategic bombers violates our territorial space, we'll shoot it down without a problem."

General Martel tapped his fingers on the table. "And if it carried a thermonuclear bomb? What then?"

"Putin will call right away to apologize, saying the plane went off route. Like he always does." General Sanchez scowled. "He could even blame us for it, asking why we shot it down, saying we should have called him. But what are we supposed to do in a situation like this, bring about a reciprocal nuclear blow?"

"Sounds like he's trying to turn the Crimean peninsula into his unsinkable aircraft carrier," said General Martel.

Admiral Adams opened the dossier on the table in front of him, then snapped it shut in disgust. "Bollocks! The Crimean peninsula is already bursting with Russian special forces and Kadirov's Chechens. Those men have developed one hell of a ruthless operation and are ready to use their experiences in Crimea."

John spoke above the murmurs and whispers erupting around the table. "Gentlemen, in the next few days, Putin will send 20,000 more soldiers to Crimea to provoke an armed conflict. He wants Ukraine to fire first so he can proceed without limit. He wants to turn Ukraine into the next Chechnya."

"And the Ukrainian army?" General Martel asked. "Can they not offer any kind of resistance?"

"Highly unlikely," John said. "Ukraine's new government can't control its armed forces. Never mind the total corruption of the political and military circles, the Russian secret services have complete control over Ukrainian troops."

"So Ukraine doesn't have the slightest chance of defending Crimea," General Sanchez said.

Admiral Adams pounded his fist on the table. "We've already forgiven Russia for two wars in the Caucuses. Maybe that was our mistake? Maybe that's why he feels relaxed now, unpunished and inspired, behaving like he owns both worlds—the Black Sea and the Sea of Azov."

General Martel clicked his tongue against his teeth. "Why is Putin so determined to hold on to Ukraine?"

Once again, everyone turned to John, waiting for some insight. John leaned forward, placing his elbows on the table and lacing his fingers together.

"You are most likely familiar with Otto von Bismarck—German ambassador to Russia from 1859 to 1862 and a talented politician who understood Russia's strengths and weaknesses. Well, there is a saying attributed to him, that goes, 'The power of Russia could be undermined only by separating Ukraine from it…Ukraine should not only be torn away from Russia but also set against it. We should play off one part of the single nation against the other and watch one brother kill the other.'"

John sat back in his chair. "Whether Bismarck actually said this is unimportant. It remains true. Without realizing it, Putin is fulfilling Bismarck's prophetic words. Nobody has put these two nations at each other's throats as well as he has since Crimea's annexation. He's the architect of Russia's tragic destiny."

"Did he really need to brew up such a storm? Where is he trying to get to in such a hurry?" Admiral Adams murmured.

John smiled. "Surely you remember Leonid Shebarshin?"

The Admiral groaned. "Former Chief of Soviet external intelligence. Pain in my backside."

John nodded. "He once said, 'Russians quickly harness horses but never ride in the right direction.'"

The men around the table laughed again, this time louder and with mounting, palpable tension.

"We are on the threshold of a global event in Eastern Europe," John said. "We don't know which way Russians will go. They themselves don't even know where fortune will take them. Gentlemen, we must take all measures, use all of our resources, use our diplomatic channels and secret services in Ukraine and in Russia to prevent World War Three."

CHAPTER 2

John turned off the TV and picked up his phone, dialing the number from memory. He was about to hang up after the fifth ring when he heard someone answer on the other end.

"This had better be important. You're interrupting my fishing day."

John bit back a laugh. The tightness in Tom's voice suggested that he was not catching many fish, which meant that it was a typical day of fishing for him.

"Did you listen to the news on your way out to the lake?"

Tom sighed loudly. "You know I left politics."

"We need your help." John tapped his fingers on the counter, waiting for Tom to respond.

"I've got nothing to do with that nonsense anymore."

"When the conflict between Russia and Ukraine grows into a full-scale war, then we, along with all of Western Europe, will be pulled into this shit."

Tom chuckled into the phone. "Sharon and I are well into World War IV. Tonight will not be my first sleeping in the boat."

"Jesus, is it really that bad?" John ran a hand through his hair. "Can't you just calm down and return home?"

"I'm scared."

"Of what—Sharon?"

"No." Tom cleared his throat. "Of surrender."

"Yours or Sharon's?"

"As if Sharon would ever give up."

"Yea, yea, you're right, Tom." John chuckled. "I also remember how quickly Sharon made you surrender during that martial art competition at college. Should have known it was the final victory."

Without giving a chance for Tom to reply he added:

"Listen, get your ass home and get cleaned up. I've got to head into the White House for a bit, but I'll swing by your place tonight. We'll celebrate the armistice—Sharon will be happy with your surrender. But I need to talk to you."

"Don't say I didn't warn you about the unpleasantness."

"Speaking of unpleasantness," John said, happy for the chance to change topics, "what do you think about Putin? Surely you were able to study him better than anyone else when you were in Russia."

"You're asking the wrong person," Tom said quickly. "Call Bush Jr. He's the only one I knew who was able to look into Putin's eyes and understand his soul. I can neither see nor understand that which does not exist."

"Oh, come on . . ." John rolled his eyes.

"Or call McCain in Arizona. Of course, when he looked into Putin's eyes, he saw three famous letters: KGB. Personally, I think that's closer to the truth."

John exhaled slowly through his teeth. "McCain would be more interested in what time we were going to nuke the Kremlin."

"If I were in his spot, I would ask you the same exact thing." After a few seconds, Tom spoke again, his voice barely a whisper now. "John, they're biting."

The line went dead, and John shook his head, hoping his friend caught at least one fish before the sun went down. It would put him in a much better mood.

At seven o'clock sharp, John stepped out of his dark sedan, clutching several gifts for his host, and jogged up the steps to Tom and Sharon's home—a Victorian-style mini-mansion. It was still a respectable size and had more space than John would care to be responsible for, but Tom and Sharon were known for entertaining.

The door swung open to reveal an elegantly dressed Sharon, her black hair pulled back in a loose bun. She had dark eyes that seemed to shift in the light of the entryway, and an angular face that was becoming more distinguished as the years went on. "John," she said with evident pleasure, "what a *surprise*! Come on in."

"A surprise?" John asked as he stepped across the threshold, holding a bouquet of fresh roses and a small paper bag with a fine Georgian wine and her favorite cake.

A large rumbling sounded, and he turned to see Tom's Jeep whip into the drive and pause in front of the garage door, waiting for it to raise high enough for him to drive inside.

Sharon crossed her arms and spoke through clenched teeth. "Always making an entrance at the last moment." She glanced at John and, as if just noticing him, immediately put the mask of pleasant hostess back into place. "Ever the strategist," she said, accepting his gifts.

The armistice was a success, and soon the three of them were seated around a cozy table tucked into a room just off the kitchen. The table was covered with a large platter of fresh-baked fish surrounded by smaller plates of salads and sweets. The cake, nearly empty bottle of wine, and fragrant roses rounded out the family-style atmosphere.

John was just about to launch into the real reason he'd travelled to the suburbs when a joyful childish cry echoed from the staircase. Kevin, Sharon and Tom's eight-year-old grandson raced into the room and hugged Tom tightly, rejoicing that his grandpa had returned. When Sharon cleared her throat, Kevin looked up at her, then turned to John, stretching out a hand shyly, but respectfully.

"Nice to see you again, Mr. John."

John shook the proffered hand, then pretended as if Kevin's grip was painful. "Such a strong man you've become, Kevin." He winced overdramatically, which made Kevin giggle and Sharon frown. "What grade are you in now?

"Second."

"And did you just get out of school at this late hour?"

Kevin tried to maintain a straight face, but giggled again. "I was watching TV."

"Movie or cartoons?"

Sharon cleared he throat. "The History Channel."

Kevin leaned closer to John to share a secret. "They were talking about Dracula."

"Dracula?" John inquired with feigned confusion. "Is that some kind of animal?"

Tom hid a laugh while Kevin nodded excitedly. "Yeah, sorta. But on two feet with a human face. He's also called Vlad the Third, or Son of the Devil, because he always desired human blood and—"

"Kevin," Sharon interrupted quickly, "you can tell Mr. John about Dracula another time. For now, go and get ready for bed."

Kevin waved goodbye and jumped up the stairs, two at a time. When they heard the door close upstairs, Sharon turned to John, her lips pursed and her eyebrows raised.

"So, the Russian–Ukrainian crisis. That is the purpose of your visit, is it not?"

John and Tom exchanged uncomfortable looks.

"I knew it," she continued. "Don't even think about suggesting that we return to Russia. We gave her almost twenty years. And do you know what the most difficult moment was?"

John spread his arms out before him.

"Sharon, to be honest, I don't know and will not even attempt to guess. I only know one thing, from personal experience: that a spy's whole life has to do with risk and stress. With unpredictability and a whole row of other difficulties."

Sharon held up a hand to stop him. "Forgive me friend, but you are incorrect. Everything that you have listed was for me just the work environment. I will tell you plainly, the hardest moment, or more accurately, the most *painful* moment of all the years we worked in Russia was when I was watching on the Moscow News how Putin rewarded his secret services agents with ornaments and medals, while at the same time your administration crucified our secret services for all of our dedication and unconditional devotion to our country."

She shook her head, the pain and frustration rushing back to her, as sharp as if it were yesterday. "This was too painful for words. We have placed our very best and the most precious years of our lives on the map of destiny. We did this only out of love for America, for peace and the safety of our county. And what did we get in return? A cross and nails."

"Sharon, years have gone by. Let's not talk about this. Don't take it personally—approach it professionally. It was just politics. Maybe the new administration didn't understand all the details of your, I mean, our work…please accept my sincerest apology for all of us. The latest events have shown how naïve we were in trusting the Russians. They lied to us…"

"And you, after all these years of working in the Department of Defense, still have not learned the simplest truth. When has the Kremlin ever spoken the truth? You may think I am naïve, but you are the ones who forget who are dealing with so easily."

"Sharon, we've learned our lesson. Let's believe that the mistakes of the past will become good lessons in the future."

"I hope so! But nothing has changed." Sharon grinned sarcastically, then lowered her voice. With deep bitterness she added, "The Kremlin is always lying, and we are always trying to find some way of believing them. So tell me, if we don't understand are we optimistic, or just foolish?"

"Let's move forward. Let's hear him out before we decide," Tom said diplomatically, his eyes fixed on his hands, swirling a wine glass on the table. Sharon rolled her eyes before turning to John, waiting for him to continue.

John considered his words carefully. Finally, he decided the direct approach would work best with Sharon, as she was clearly in the position to make any final decisions. "Your extensive work in Russia and close ties with Putin's circles would give you access to what we need most."

"Which is?" Sharon asked.

"Who controls the Kremlin, him or the oligarchs? Can he actually launch nuclear weapons? Is he capable of starting a nuclear holocaust?"

Tom looked up at his wife. "I have no doubt that his staff has explained how nuclear weapons would affect all of us, not just one side."

"And if he doesn't understand that?" John asked quietly.

"You know more than enough about Putin. What do you think?"

"Yes, I do know who he is, but that's not enough to create a full profile of his personality. I need to know much more about him. I need to know not just who he is, but who he was."

Tom shifted in his seat, considering his next words. "Putin once worked in Germany. Of course, it was all bullshit, but the media tried to create the illusion of a mysterious, modern spy-president. Of course, no one mentions that a two-hour interview would result in only a few fragments being authorized by Putin—the ones that made him look like a superman." He paused to finish off his glass of wine. "After Germany, he was called to Leningrad, to a university, to watch over the foreign students and read over the professors' oaths to one another. It should have meant the end of his KGB career, if it weren't for Sobchak, his former teacher."

"You're getting ahead of yourself, dear."

Tom offered a thankful nod to his wife before continuing.

"Putin went to Dresden after he completed the Moscow Institute Andropov, where he studied under the pseudonym Platov. He was sent to this KGB school in 1984 ranking as a Major, and spent only one year there. He specialized in German-speaking countries such as Austria and Switzerland. He worked as Director of the Home of Soviet–German friendship. Of course, he also watched over Soviet students in East Germany, monitored anticommunist protests in Germany, and hosted and entertained generals from Moscow. He would load them into the plane if they couldn't get in themselves after overdosing on vodka.

"But he was not sinless, even back then. He had unauthorized contact with representatives of the Mossad's intelligence network and, in 1990, he was called back to Leningrad. His career should have ended, but the criminal city of St. Petersburg met him with open arms and helped him hone his skill of combining corruption, crime, and the connections and influence of the secret services for all possible illegal financial operations. He surrounded himself with people not afraid to get involved in anything—drugs, corruption, or even the fate of elderly Leningrad citizens who endured the blockade during the war…"

Sharon cleared her throat. "I think you're losing John. Get to the point, dear."

Tom leaned forward on his arms on the table. "In the early 1990s, Leningrad's grocery stores were completely empty. The elderly who survived the war were remembering the German blockade of 1941–1944 with tears in their eyes, especially now that they were once again seeing the streets of Leningrad littered with starved corpses."

"Jesus," John whispered.

"Sobchak was Mayor of Leningrad at the time. After Putin was fired from the KGB in 1991, Sobchak appointed him Chairman of the city's external affairs committee. They didn't care about the rampant hunger. They feared a coup. They opened up storehouses of goods on army bases, but it was too little, too late. Sobchak turned to world leaders for help, and humanitarian aid poured in, including from our own military bases."

Tom offered John and Sharon more wine, but both declined. He emptied the bottle into his glass and drank half of it before speaking again.

"At that time, we could have easily bought the Russian army and turned Russia into our fifty-first state. But we acted with understanding. Sobchak kept the aid a secret, and we indulged his lies. Everyone understood that he was afraid for his reputation and position. Meanwhile, Putin controlled the exchange of Russia's raw resources. He exported everything—valuable metals, oil, forestry products—anything he could get his hands on. In return, Leningrad was supposed to be receiving food products. But only a small portion of food came in, just enough not to raise suspicions. The rest was converted to currency. Putin was discovered, but instead of going to prison, he got a promotion."

"All hail Mother Russia," Sharon said, the sarcasm thick in her voice.

"In 1992, he led St. Petersburg's delegation to Frankfurt, where he and another delegation member persuaded a group of Frankfurt investors to create the German company SPAG to deal with St. Petersburg real estate. When Putin was appointed Prime Minister in 1999, Germany officially opened a criminal case on the company. Company officials were charged with laundering money for Russian criminal groups and Columbian drug dealers." Tom look at John and raised an eyebrow. "Putin remained a freelance advisor to SPAG until March 2000. When he became president, he tried—and succeeded to some extent—to buy all of the documentation from the Germans."

"But copies remain," Sharon interrupted. "Ukrainian security services have some of the originals as well."

Surprised, John said, "I didn't know you worked in Ukraine." Sharon simply shrugged in response.

"It was our naivety that helped them." Tom leaned back and looked up at the ceiling. "In March 1992, I got a call from a colleague in MI-6 who told me they had detained one of my 'wards' at Heathrow."

"Putin?" John asked.

Tom looked at John and frowned in disgust. "Sobchak. With more than a million dollars in cash. Yeltsin intervened, and they released him, but it didn't stop Sobchak, Putin, and their circle from taking money out of Russia to buy vacation homes in different countries. Spanish secret services determined that they transferred over twenty million dollars into Spain alone during a two-year period. So more than two decades ago, Russia already recognized the corruption of both Putin and Sobchak. Those twenty million, were just the beginning of their criminal Journey."

"And Yeltsin's administration still took him in."

They all sat in silence for a moment, letting John's words sink in.

Tom went on, "Yeltsin never saw him as his successor, you know. He expected the young mayor of Novgorod, Boris Nemtsov, to take his place. Even told Clinton, Kohl, and other leaders so. But when Yeltsin was running for his second term. Nemtsov demanded he end the war in Chechnya."

"Which Yeltsin ultimately did," John said, interrupting.

"Yes, but Nemtsov was a man of uncompromising principle, which alarmed Yeltsin He needed a successor who could guarantee his safety, not throw him out like he did Gorbachev."

"Or toss him in jail," Sharon added.

John nodded in understanding. "And Putin was the complete opposite of Nemtsov."

"Yeltsin needed to get rid of anyone who might disrupt his peaceful retirement," Tom said. "Putin promised to do this, but he needed authority."

"So Yeltsin made him director of the KGB," John said.

"FSB by that time," Sharon corrected him. She picked up a forked and played with a half-eaten piece of cake on her plate, but didn't eat any more.

"You see, Putin is a master of 'soft power.'"

John nodded as Tom spoke.

"He understands the power of money, and how to manipulate religions and the press. And when the real test of his loyalty came in 1998 and 1999, when Russia's Attorney General authorized a number of corruption cases affecting Yeltsin's inner circle. Putin gave us a glimpse of the sort of leader he would become—releasing a sex tape to discredit the man."

"A sex tape." Sharon chuckled. "No points for creativity on that one."

"But it worked," John pointed out.

"That it did," Sharon conceded.

"When the Attorney General still refused to back down, Putin played the tape on Russian television. Even had his experts 'authenticate' it."

John snorted. "Convenient."

"And effective," Tom added. "Yeltsin publically announced Putin as his successor and the Duma approved."

The Duma was part of the ruling assembly in Russia at the time, with ties to Soviet-era legislative bodies. "I'm sure it didn't hurt that so many in the Duma were involved in Putin's deeds," John said.

"Not at all," Sharon said. "And Putin fulfilled his promise and signed a decree granting total immunity for Yeltsin and his entire family. The problem was that barely anyone in the nation *knew* Putin, but here was Yeltsin, asking the people to vote for this unknown—a person whose presidential rating at the time was only one percent. Putin needed a way to stir up Russians' passions. Chechnya was back on the political world map, but Putin needed the people to demand action rather than just initiating it on his own. As if on cue, terrorists attacked Buynaksk, Moscow, and Volgodonsk, killing hundreds and injuring thousands more. The Kremlin blamed the Chechen terrorists.

"Who were never found," Tom pointed out.

"Are you surprised?" John asked, his own question full of cynicism.

"But everything blew up in their faces—excuse the pun," Sharon said, "when people observed FSB trying to blow up a building in Ryazan. They failed and tried to write it off as anti-terror exercises, but everyone knew they were lying."

"And that's when the Russian mass media stepped up, and in a matter of hours, anti-Chechen hysteria swept across Russia." Tom held up his half-empty wine glass. "So began the second Chechen war." He drained the glass.

"And tens of thousands of barbarous deaths were placed at the feet of Putin's throne," Sharon said.

The three of them sat in silence for several moments. Finally, John spoke.

"And we let it happen."

"We let this little Kremlin rivulet turn into an ocean of blood," Tom said. "Putin's opponents, journalists, Russian officers—whether from assassination or an epidemic of suicides, people were dropping like flies. Even Sobchak was not immune."

"Which is what makes it so dangerous for him to have access to nuclear weapons," John said, suddenly excited that Tom had made his point for him. "Will he take such a step in Ukraine?"

Tom picked up a small piece of bread and chewed on it thoughtfully while the others waited for his response. Finally he shrugged. "I can't answer with confidence, but I will say this: Before his presidency, he was never direct or decisive. He's a good manipulator who bluffs well."

"Let him take Crimea," Sharon said suddenly. When John stared at her incredulously, she added, "It's inevitable."

"But not for a thank you," Tom said. "He's a professional criminal. You need to act nontraditionally as well."

"What, tell the Ukrainian military not to resist? Just fling open the doors and let the wolf in?"

Sharon stood to clear several plates. "The Ukrainians have no real army. If Putin provokes them into firing first, it will begin a full-scale invasion of Ukraine. Nobody needs that."

"Nobody needs that," Tom repeated.

"Just give up Crimea to the Russians," John said, more to himself, still disbelieving this recommendation. How would he ever convince NATO to accept this option?

Sharon returned from the kitchen. "Under the right circumstances, Crimea can become for Russia what the Trojan horse became for Troy. The first day of the annexation of Crimea could be the last day for all of Putin's hallucinations of a great Russian empire."

John folded his arms and leaned back in his chair. He licked his lips several times, trying to find the right words. "At the last NATO meeting, I was asked to find someone close to Putin's circle and the nuclear generals. I'm sure you can appreciate that, given the current situation, we have to keep the slightest whispers or rustlings in the Kremlin under control." He looked up at Tom.

"We're retired," Sharon said forcefully.

John and Tom continued staring at each other in an uneasy silence. John knew that "ex-spies" were a myth. Once in the game, someone was always in it.

"We are retired," Sharon said again, this time a hint of fear entering her voice.

Tom finally broke the stare off and turned to Sharon, although his words were directed at John.

"Professor Usachev. He's physicist. He has very good ties with Kremlin generals and admirals—he was working with the Russian Ministry of Defense at the time.

Sharon sank into her seat, her face deathly white.

"Where did you find him?" John asked.

"He found me." Tom said quietly.

"I went out for lunch once when I was at the Embassy in Moscow. As soon as I finished parking my car, an unassuming elderly man parked his old Lada right in front of me. There were several open spots around me, but I didn't think much about it at the time."

"Perhaps you we're getting a little too comfortable," John said sarcastically.

"Perhaps," Tom responded with a halfhearted smile.

"We walked into the restaurant at about the same time. However, he left a bit earlier than I did. He was already sitting in his car when I came out and, before I could even open my door, he started backing up and hit my car!"

"I was stunned by the sloppiness of this old man. Frustratingly stunned," Tom said with an exhale.

"God, I would have been ready to lay into him," John murmured.

"Oh, I'm sure Tom was ready to as well," Shared added.

"Yes, but he quickly walked out from his car and immediately began apologizing. He tried to do it in English, but I responded to him in Russian, telling him this wasn't necessary."

"The old man looked deep into my eyes as I was talking. At that moment I knew that this wasn't an accident. He asked me to come to his car so that he could give me his insurance information."

"When I came to his car, he opened the glove compartment and pulled out a folded piece of paper. The smell of Vodka came from his breath. I asked him if was drunk or if he needed some help."

"Don't worry," the old man said with a stern and sober gaze

"Once you unfold this paper you'll likely drink from the same well," he said half-jokingly.

"But do not open this paper until you will get to your office. This will be better for both of us."

"So what was in that paper?" John asked.

"There was information about who this man is and details about the projects that he was managing for the Russian military," Tom explained.

"I met with him a few times in Novosibirsk. He lived there. But after a while I lost all contact with him, and he appears to have disappeared. Sharon and I retired soon after. Until now we don't know what happened to this old man—Professor Usachev."

For a few moments everybody was silent.

Finally John looked back to Tom. "It looks to me like you had an Ace in your pocket. Is there any way to get it back?"

Tom silently looked down to the floor.

Sharon fidgeted with her napkin, refusing to look up from the table. She understood Tom's feelings and, before he answered, she looked up at John and asked, "How long will you take him away from me?" Her voice was hoarse, barely audible.

"I don't know," John said. "But the sooner we leave, the sooner I can get him back to you."

The evening ended soon after, and John took his leave. The entire drive home he replayed the conversation in his mind. He tried imagining how he would ever convince NATO or the Ukrainian government to simply let Crimea go without a fight, but the words would not come to him. He was only a few blocks from his home when he decided to head back into the office instead, hoping his research might inspire him.

He was on his second pot of particularly black coffee when his phone rang, startling him. He glanced at the clock and frowned. Good news never came at 5:30 in the morning. The caller ID showed Tom and Sharon's number.

He answered. "What happened?"

"We're in the hospital. It's Tom—he got all gung-ho about preparing for the trip and then . . . damn you, John. I'm putting this on your shoulders."

John's stomach lurched. "What happened?" he said again, his mouth suddenly dry.

"Heart attack."

"I'll be there in thirty minutes."

When John entered the hospital room, Sharon was sitting close to the bed, her hand draped across Tom's forehead. Her eyes were ringed in red. Tom's face was drawn and pale. His eyes were closed.

John walked to the side of the bed. "How is he?" he asked in a whisper.

"Fine." Tom answered, barely moving his lips. He opened his eyes, looked at John, and with the tiniest note of sarcasm added, "I hope this is not the work of Putin."

John bit his bottom lip to keep from laughing too loudly.

"I seem to have overdone it a bit," Tom said, trying to sit up. Sharon tapped his shoulder and gave him a pointed look, and he relaxed back down to his original position.

"I should be the one apologizing," John said. "Sometimes I forget that we are not the indestructible Marines of our youth."

"Puts a major kink in your plans," Tom said.

John sighed and sank into a chair by the foot of the bed. "Maybe you know someone from your past who could step in?"

Tom looked at Sharon, a question hanging between the two of them.

She scowled at him, then leaned over to kiss him quickly. When she stood back up, she spoke in a demanding tone. "Promise me that you will look after Kevin—better than you look after yourself."

"Of course."

"Promise me!"

"I promise, I promise."

John looked from Tom to Sharon and back again. "Wait, what's going on?"

Tom smiled weakly. "Meet my replacement." Sharon held out a hand.

Shocked, John opened his mouth to remind Sharon that she didn't even want Tom to go, but then he thought better of it. "What changed?"

Sharon straightened her shoulders. "Patriotism calls."

"But will you be able–?"

She held up a hand to stop him, smiling as if about to reveal a secret. "When the devil cannot handle a matter, he sends a woman to do the work."

~CHAPTER 3~

Yalta

Before the Russian occupation of the Crimean peninsula and its transformation into a launching pad for Russian nuclear missiles, strategic bombers, submarines, and various types of ships, Yalta had been a great resort area on the Black Sea coast. Her doors had always open to all nations—and of course thousands of lovers. The hot Crimean sun, the mesmerizing sound of waves, the soft sand, the rustle of the palm trees, the music from restaurants open late into the night, the starry sky, and the vibrant setting of the moon pulled all visitors into the mysterious world of romance.

But that was then. . .

Tatyana looked down at her watch. It was already 10:00 PM, and her evening had yet to become romantic. She turned off the floor lamp, placed the newspaper on the table, and made her way to the television. There was an energetic bounce in her step, partially impatience and partially her natural inclination. She had brown hair that fell around her shoulders like falling leaves, and a soft, intelligent face. She stopped near the bookshelf. At first she wanted to take a book, but her arm reached to the pile of DVDs. She looked through her small collection and pulled one out. Smirking, she inserted the disc into the player.

Before she had time to turn the DVD player, the doorbell rang, the sound mimicking a parrot saying, "guest, guest, guest; guest, guest, guest."

"Finally!" She rubbed her palms and half-jumped, half-danced to the door, which she opened as slowly as possible.

A pleasant baritone rose up from behind the door. "What are you doing? Is the door stuck or something?"

Tatyana jerked the door open to reveal a dark-haired man with a slim, athletic figure. His determined look, subtle smile, and tailored light gray suit gave him an unusual aristocratic presence, the kind that in this day and age she'd only read about in books. An expensive box of chocolates and a lovely carnation emphasized his aristocracy, proving that he was a sweet gentleman who knew how to appreciate the female gender.

"Dear, what's wrong with you? Let me inside."

"You can wait," Tanya answered in a playful, sing-song voice, resting her palm on his chest. Her other hand went to her hip. "First of all, don't call me 'dear.'"

The man's blue eyes flashed as he looked at her with a slight wariness.

"Not dear," she repeated. She lifted her hand from her hip and tapped her lips with one finger, as if searching for the right word. "Comrade Commander—I believe that's how you guys say it, right?"

"Specifically, Comrade Commander *in Chief!*"

"And since I am chief now, where are your apologies for being late, Lieutenant Colonel?"

He snapped his heels together. "Apologies for being late, ma'am!"

"I'm not joking around."

He stepped into the room, and removed her hand from his chest as he placed the flowers and chocolates down on a small table. In one fluid motion, he grabbed her graceful waist, and swung her off the ground like a feather. "Would you just let me inside already, Comrade in Chief?" He kicked the door shut behind him, walked to the window, and lowered her feet to the ground before kissing her on the cheek. He turned and gathered up his offerings, the presented her with the box of candies and purple carnation. "This is for you, the always commanding one—unless you have more orders for me?"

"Yes, of course, Comrade Ivanov. To the kitchen—double time!"

"And off I go." Alexander headed to the kitchen, dropping his coat and tie on the sofa before rolling up his sleeves. "Do you have anything I can snack on?"

"Everything that you find is yours." She plopped into a chair and took the candies from the box. "I think I already found something for myself."

Alexander slammed several cabinets. "You don't have anything here!"

"I didn't say I had anything to eat." She giggled. "I just said whatever you found was yours."

Alexander appeared in the kitchen doorway, frowning. "Fine, get dressed and we'll head to the city for dinner."

"To the city, to the city," Tanya muttered. "You can't do that, you know. I waited more than two hours for you. You couldn't call? Or did you forget my number?"

"I called you several times!"

Tanya pointed at the table. "My cell phone has been quiet all night."

Alexander grabbed the cell phone, flipped it open, and grinned. "You know these things only work if you keep the battery charged."

Tatyana jumped up from the chair and grabbed the phone from him. The screen was indeed black. "Well, damn." She looked down at her t-shirt and faded pants. "Now I guess I have to apologize for not being dressed for the occasion."

"No apologies necessary. Let's just grab something quick on the waterfront. "

"No way, Comrade Officer. To reward you for your patience and understanding, I'm about to present you with a governmental award." She rubbed her hands together and smiled.

"And what would that be exactly?"

"Pilimeni followed by vareniki and sausage along with some salad. Finally, and most importantly, a glass of Black Doctor."

"And where do you keep all of these rewards? Your kitchen holds nothing but an old bottle of milk, some loaves of bread, and a few cakes."

Tatyana nodded toward the corner, where two big bags were standing.

"Oops," Alexander said as he moved over to the bags. "I failed to notice the elephant in the room."

"I knew my refrigerator was empty, so I picked up some supplies—although a walk on the waterfront in the fresh air sounds nice. If only you hadn't arrived so late." She affected a playful pout.

"Sorry, my dear. I had to stop by Simferopol."

"You mean that you drove from Sevastopol to Yalta through Simferopol?"

"That's right, Comrade Commander. And from there, I came straight to you." He pulled her into a hug.

"Yes, a decent hook. What did you do with your uniform? Did you leave it in the car or something?"

"No, in Sevastopol."

She stepped back from him. "You were on duty in civilian clothing? You've been walking around in civilian clothing a lot more often recently. Are you going AWOL, Alex dear?"

"Tanya, if this version makes our evening more romantic, I accept it without any resistance. But why have we only talked about me? What's going on with you?" He pointed to the still-open DVD player. "What are we watching?"

"I wanted to watch *The Sound of Music*, but you rang the doorbell just as I was putting it in." She looked up at him. "For some reason, while I was waiting for you, something made me want to watch it again."

"Hit play and we'll have our own night at the movies." Alexander made himself comfortable on the sofa. Before Tatyana could turn on the DVD, Alexander's phone rang. He glanced at the number. "Don't turn it on yet," he said as he walked back into the kitchen.

Tatyana sat down in a chair. Only a few whispered phrases reached her ears.

"Yalta... But we agreed that I'm free until tomorrow... Who, the general or the admiral? I know them, but not personally ... Right now? Okay. I'm heading out."

Alexander returned to the living room to find Tatyana staring at the black TV screen without blinking. They both knew their romantic evening had ended before it had even begun. He lifted her chin so he could look into her eyes. "I'm sorry–"

She pulled away from him and dug through the bags, pulling out a small container and a bottle of wine. "At least take a couple of dumplings for the road. Maybe a sip of wine?"

Alex shook his head. "No wine. I'm about to drive. Plus I'm already on duty. But I'll gladly take some dumplings. Maybe some sausages as well?"

She put together a small dish of food for him. "You'll be alright, yes? I know it's not the time to ask questions, but with everything happening in Crimea and Sevastopol, the riots and soldiers. . ." She let her voice trail off.

He hugged her from behind, whispering into her ear, "Stay at home."

"How about I come visit you in Sevastopol over the weekend?"

"Home—work, work—home. Don't go shopping unless it's absolutely necessary. Understood?"

"Ugh, work. It's not like I understand anything that's going on anyway." She spun around to face him. "I just don't know who to trust. Some say one thing, the others something else. And then this Putin came out of nowhere." She looked up into Alex's eyes. "Yesterday, my friend Dinara, she is a Tartar, told me that in the city of Alushta, the Russian priests threw out all Ukrainian items from the church and they don't allow the Ukrainians to come in to pray. We never had this happen before they came. We never used to distinguish between Russian, Ukrainian, Tartar, or Jewish people, but now our editorial department can't seem to agree on anything. I want to figure it out for myself. So dear, whether you like it or not, expect me to come visit you."

Alex's voice was more forceful when he spoke. "It's not safe. In fact, it's highly risky."

Tatyana rose up on her tippy toes, gently kissed him, and whispered in his ear, "If you can take risks, then why deprive me of the same pleasure? Risk is my middle name." She stepped back from him and almost laughed at his expression. She opened the door for him. "Don't be offended. I'll try to not be sarcastic anymore—at least not today. And regarding Sevastopol," she added in a serious tone, "I think that we'll see each other there. I want to know the real situation."

Alexander hugged her, kissed her, and—without looking back—ran down the steps to his car.

CHAPTER 4

Sevastopol

Alexander stepped deliberately along the path to the Russian Black Sea Fleet Headquarters. The attendant stopped him and asked for identification. Alexander was in civilian clothing, after all. He dug his ID out of his coat pocket and presented it. Seeing the identification, the attendant saluted him. "Comrade Lieutenant Colonel, General Trofimov is waiting for you."

Alexander entered the large, characterless building. After going up several flights of steps, he arrived at the General's offices. The reception desk was empty. Alexander knocked on the heavy wooden door and, without waiting for an answer, opened it.

The salt-and-pepper-haired General was sitting at the table. Turning away from the computer, he looked Alexander up and down, and said, "Come in. Sit down." He pointed to a chair next to his desk. "I see that you didn't sleep either."

Alexander offered a questioning look.

"Red eyes," the General said. "Don't relax just yet. The situation in Crimea and Sevastopol is changing hourly. We know that Kiev is following the US and NATO's instructions. They want to hold on to Crimea and the military facilities for as long as they can, but without the use of weapons. They figured out our plans, which means it's unlikely that we'll be able to provoke them to open fire first."

"They're forcing us to play their cards," Alexander said.

"And now if we open fire first, what comes next may be unpredictable and cost us too much on the international stage, as well as within the country. We must use everything to destabilize Kiev—and if possible, all of Ukraine—at the hands of the Ukrainians themselves. These obstinate Ukrainians smell of the West. Marshal Zhukov was right…"

"Zhukov?" Alexander prompted.

"During the World War II battles in Ukraine, near Kiev. Zhukov said: 'the more Ukrainians that will drown in the Dnieper River, the fewer we'll have to send to Siberia.' These shrewd Ukrainians, they were never ours, and it looks like they never will be. You should know your history better." He scowled. "In a couple of days, Turchinov becomes Commander in Chief of Ukraine's armed forces, and yesterday we learned that Berezovsky was appointed Commander of the Black Sea Fleet. Moscow wants us to recruit him."

"Do we have any dirt on him?"

"They said they'd get everything ready. But in this case, it is not so much about compromise, as it is about time. Just a few hours ago, our radio intelligence intercepted a conversation, or rather a confrontation, between Berezovsky and Kiev."

The General's phone rang. Alexander stood to step out, but the General motioned for him to stay. "He's in my office right now," the General said into the phone. "I think he'll orient himself all right. He's a professional." A few second later, he hung up. He thought for a moment before saying, "That was Moscow. Berezovsky is no longer Commander. He will officially be fired tomorrow. They want you to recruit him immediately."

Alexander could barely restrain his grin. "Seems some substantial dirt on Berezovsky fell into Kiev's hands. Have any of ours recruited him before?"

"As far as I know, no. According to intelligence reports, the dismissal is due to 'the inability to organize command of the troops in extreme conditions.'"

Alexander leaned forward, placing his elbows on his knees. "But does Berezovsky himself know that he has already been fired?"

The General scowled again and shook his head. "Kiev will tell him tomorrow. What does this give us?"

"Well, it doesn't make sense to recruit a 'former' Commander. But he still has a few hours in his career. We can take advantage of this."

The General pushed back in his chair, a sour look on his face. "Why do we need him? Why publicly shame the Russian fleet with this mediocrity? I don't know what Moscow is thinking."

"You're right, sir, we don't need him. However, given the situation on the peninsula, his title and position could be something we can use to discredit and demoralize the Ukrainian army."

"Then go find him." The general slapped his desk. "I'll send a few of our men to help you."

Alexander stood. "Would it be possible to send a copy of the recordings of Kiev's conversations regarding his dismissal to my phone? It will help me to be more influential and effective. I'll only have a few minutes for recruitment."

The General nodded and dismissed Alexander, who headed directly to the headquarters of the Naval Forces of Ukraine.

Sevastopol is a historic city. It played a key role in the Crimean War, and was ultimately sacked by the French, British, and Turks. The Russians lost control of the city in 1855. Few cities on earth are as steeped in military history as Sevastopol, something Alexander kept in mind as he made his way to the Naval headquarters. When Alexander arrived, Berezovsky was not there. His phone rang a few minutes later, and he was told that Berezovsky was at a restaurant near the monument to the lost ships. He was dining with three others.

"Reserve me a table next to them and put a bug on my chair," Alexander told the FSB agent on the phone. "Keep the General up to date with the details. I won't have the time or the ability to coordinate my actions and decisions with him. I will act according to the circumstances.

At the entrance to the restaurant, an FSB officer briefed Alexander.

"How long have they been there?" Alexander asked.

"Halfway through their meal."

Alexander approached a bartender and ordered a bottle of the best wine delivered to his table. Then he went to his table. As he was passing by Berezovsky, he intentionally tripped, reaching out for the Commander's shoulder to keep his balance. All four officers jumped from their chairs.

"Guys, guys, I'm sorry," Alexander said, motioning for them to take their seats. "I pulled a muscle," he said, pointing to his leg. "This is what happens sometimes. I sincerely apologize, Comrade," Alexander said, addressing Berezovsky personally.

The Commander looked at Alexander. Alexander returned a meaningful look to Berezovsky, hoping to make a personal impression and be invited to the table. When Berezovsky finally glanced away, Alexander waived the waiter over and asked him to bring whichever meat dish took the least time to cook. Then he motioned for the bartender and instructed him to give the bottle he had ordered to the neighboring table of men, whom he'd offended. "Open the bottle yourself and pour the wine. Do not leave any chance for refusal. Your tip will be determined by the success of your service."

The conversation at the neighboring table had slowly picked back up the pace. For the most part, the officers were talking about everyday topics, but then the Commander mentioned that he had ordered some imported medicine for a relative, but had not received it yet.

The bartender approached the table, wine in hand. "Gentlemen," he politely addressed the officers. Without waiting for any questions or answers, he placed a perfectly polished silver tray in the middle of the table. The golden rays of the Crimean sun gleamed on the edges of the crystal glasses. "In honor of your special service." The bartender held out the bottle for their approval, and then skillfully poured the wine into the glasses. He placed a crystal glass with gold paintings in front of the Commander.

He accepted the glass and nodded his appreciation. "To what do we owe such special service?"

"A sign of respect and apology from your humble neighbor."
The bartender suavely nodded toward Alexander.

Alexander turned around, smiled politely, and tilted his head.
"Once again, my apologies. Just trying to redeem myself."

Berezovsky held up his glass. "The fault has been redeemed.
Come join us."

Without any hesitation, Alexander shifted his chair closer to
Berezovsky and introduced himself as a businessman engaged in
the supply of domestic and imported medicine to medical insti-
tutions. His ploy worked like a charm.

One of the officers smiled at Berezovsky. "Looks like the opportunity you were looking for has dropped right in your lap,
Comrade." He emptied his glass in one gulp and signaled for his
colleagues to leave the Commander alone with his new friend.
Berezovsky nodded his head approvingly and thanked them for
their company.

Alexander's calculations had been justified. Now that they
were alone, he could determine the results of the recruitment in
five minutes. Alexander pulled out a pen and business card from
his pocket. He handed them to the Commander. "Please write
down the name of the medicine that you need for your relative."

Berezovsky wrote down the name and gave the card back to
Alexander, who glanced at it.

"German pills, right?"

"Injections."

Alexander returned the card and pen to his pocket. "I'll get
them to you in four or five days." He held up his glass of wine in
a toast. "And congratulations on your promotion to Commander
of the Naval Forces of Ukraine."

Berezovsky hesitated before drinking his own wine. He poured more for both Alexander and himself before asking, "What 'business' are you actually involved in?"

Alexander eyed him for a moment, pretending to size the man up. "I work for the FSB and I came here to meet with you specifically. Unfortunately, after your scandalous conversation with Kiev, you have already been removed from your newly appointed position."

Berezovsky's brow furrowed in anger, a protest beginning to erupt from his lips—but then Alexander took his cell phone from his pocket, opened his copy of the recorded conversations, and handed the phone to Berezovsky. Distrust was written all over his face, but it was quickly replaced with anger again as he listened to the recording. Finally, he thrust the phone back to Alexander.

Alexander didn't ask any questions. Berezovsky's reaction had told him everything he needed to know. Now, to lay the trap. "Your dismissal does not promise you a bright future in the Ukrainian army. But I can save you from this shameful situation and keep you at the top of your game."

The Commander licked his lips. "How?"

"I speak on behalf of the Kremlin. I can offer you a very prestigious post and position in the ranks of the Russian armed forces." Alexander leaned further over the table. "The president has personally expressed his hope that you will agree. But your decision to join the military ranks of the Russian Federation must be made public before Kiev's announcement of your dismissal."

The Commander poured and downed another glass of wine. "What do you need from me?"

"Just your signature on the necessary paperwork. The General will give you more details about the process of this operation and your new position. Your salary with us will be much higher than your Ukrainian one."

And that was all it took. A few moments later, but not before the wine had been exhausted, the two men gathered their coats and left. Alexander drove them to the General's office, which was unusually lively. The receptionist quickly shuffled them in to see the General. But before they could enter, the General himself came out of his office, as a sign of respect, to personally invite Berezovsky in. The General ushered him to a chair next to his desk, where bottles of brandy and whiskey along with a few cold appetizers were already waiting for him.

"First things first," the General said, sliding several pieces of paper across his desk. "The text of the oath and some other documents, including your acceptance of Russian citizenship. You need to sign them before we proceed." The General held out a pen.

Berezovsky did not take it. "I need to talk to my family."

The General nodded in appreciation, but kept the pen held out to him. "We've taken care of them. They are completely safe. We've already ordered the injections for your relative as well."

"Thank you," Berezovsky said, but with a hint of apprehension bordering on fear starting to tighten the muscles in his jaw.

"As soon as the question of your appointment is made public, we will take you to your family," the General said quickly. "But in the current situation, safety—yours and that of your family—is our responsibility. Let's first focus on finishing what we started." He placed the pen on the papers and pushed them even closer to Berezovsky. "We'll give you some time to read through everything."

The General signaled for Alexander to follow him out of the room. He led the younger man into the hallway, closing the door softly behind them, and walked briskly down the corridor to a door marked "Special Unit." He opened it with a key produced from his pocket. "Let's speak here, away from prying ears." He pointed to a soft leather chair. "I've checked it all myself. No bugs."

"Did you use our domestic seeker?"

The General rolled his eyes. "Do I look like a madman? I got an American device from one of our guys in the foreign intelligence agency."

Alexander shook his head. "Nothing is foolproof." When the General gave him a questioning look, Alexander explained. "Eighteen months ago our technicians established a sound tunnel during the repair of sewage systems in the German Embassy in Moscow. Our guys built small, wooden, tunnel-type sewer pipes into the walls. This special kind of wood reflects and transmits sound very efficiently. Only at the end of this sound tunnel—out of reach of any seekers—did they install a microphone."

"And what is the fate of this experiment?"

"One of our own spilled the secret."

The General hissed through his teeth. "Let's hope for the best. Moscow is pleased with you. Soon Berezovsky will be the newly appointed Commander of the Naval Forces of the Autonomous Republic of Crimea."

"The naval forces of the Autonomous Republic of Crimea?" Alexander repeated sarcastically and slowly. "You mean the Commander of a fleet that never existed and probably never will?"

"The exact words used are not important." The general waved a dismissive hand. "But it sounds convincing, right? Only media we control will have access to Berezovsky's details. I want you to be in charge of all media materials prior to their publication and airing."

"And his family?" Alexander asked slowly.

"Of course everything depends on Berezovsky. To the media, his family is being protected from the Ukrainian junta threatening to endanger their lives. For us, his family is insurance." The General waited for any disagreement from Alexander, but received none. "Right, so Aksenov is coming, the Chairman of the Council of Ministers of the Autonomous Republic of Crimea. Prepare the materials for him so that he can present Berezovsky well for the press. We don't want him screwing up our work."

Alexander frowned.

"What is it?" the general asked.

Alexander hesitated as he considered how transparent he wanted to be. "I am a cadre intelligence officer who's used to working with different people and in different conditions. As a rule, these are people of value to their communities, even communities of the most criminalized society. But I wouldn't want to get dirty with the same crap as this '*Goblin*'"

"Don't get ahead of yourself. He's still the authority—at least for today," the General finished in a half-whisper.

"Racketeering, beatings, extortion, violence, rape," said Alexander, his tone escalating with suppressed frustration before he quickly caught himself. "It's demeaning to paint this mobster as an angel to the common people. It is a pity to exchange an officer's honor for such games."

"You think I enjoy dealing with this criminal trash?" The General shook his head. "We are like surgeons—blood or shit, whether it stinks or it doesn't, the operation needs to be carried out." When Alexander continued to have a sour expression on his face, the General asked, "You want me to put someone else on it?"

"I would be most grateful."

The General studied him for a moment before nodding slowly. "You have a pass on this one, but I caution you to remember your duty. You have a responsibility to protect the operation still. Don't say anything unnecessary during the live broadcast, no matter what. We can't afford for Berezovsky to go off the rails."

"Absolutely," Alexander replied.

"Moscow is relying on you for a number of special operations abroad, but first I want you to lead one of the Special Forces groups to seize Ukrainian military facilities. Your team has all been to Chechnya. Use this opportunity to learn from their experience."

"Yes, sir."

"If all goes well with Berezovsky, he'll be able to recruit his own team. You'll be included, but will take no part in the recruiting. Observe and analyze. Those are your tasks now, so you can develop an effective technique for use among the Ukrainians, and in the West. The Kremlin wants us to establish close relationships with certain terrorist organizations. Create a chain of pro-Russia groups, whether they are religious organizations, the media, and associations of scholars, veterans, or retirees. Pay special attention to student associations in different universities. This is our future."

"And if Berezovsky fails to recruit a significant portion of the Ukrainians?"

The General hesitated, then hissed through his teeth. "As much as I hate these Ukrainians, they are survivors. The government betrays them, dooms them, but they fight back. Like a flamethrower turning everyone around them into ash. If the marines tear him to pieces, we just stand on the side. We've done our job."

Hundreds of Russian special forces, Chechens, Cossacks, and various types of equipment surrounded the garrison of the Ukrainian marines. A few Ukrainian officers, accompanied by a squad of marines, exited the negotiations between Berezovsky and

Aksenov. Before Aksenov had had time to present Berezovsky, one of the marines yelled out above all others.

"Glory to Ukraine! Long live the marines! Death to the traitors!"

Machine guns pointed at both sides. Six marines covered their commanders. Two others pointed machine guns at Berezovsky and Aksenov. Aksenov's semi-raised hands began to shake. His face turned ashen, the breath of life seeming to have left him already. Berezovsky stood tall, not moving.

The seconds ticked by like an eternity. Finally, one of the marines lifted a hand to the barrel of a Sergeant's machine gun and gently pushed it toward the ground. The others followed suit. The Russians lowered their machine guns as well.

Berezovsky inhaled with a jerk. He opened to mouth to speak, but the marine put his finger to his mouth, signaling for Berezovsky to keep his thoughts to himself. The marine took a few steps toward Berezovsky and Aksenov and loudly said, "A Crimean admiral without a navy is like a captain without a ship. Let's get you out of here. The sooner we do, the better it'll be for everyone."

"And just who the hell are you?" Aksenov yelled.

The marine bristled at the reproach. "Tell your Putin that the first day of the occupation of Crimea became the first day of the collapse of his empire. Soon Ukraine will be reunited in a way never seen before. Remember the Ukrainian proverb: 'the earth cannot be fooled, what you sow is what you will reap.'" He gave his soldiers the command to block the gates of the Ukrainian base and put the equipment in a circle.

Alexander watched from his stance in front of an APC. When the marine disappeared around the corner of the building, Alexander looked to Berezovsky. Their eyes met, but Berezovsky quickly looked away. Alexander turned to the APC, where the driver was waiting for him.

ᕲCHAPTER 5ᕲ

Yalta

"Alex, turn off the TV," Tatyana whined. "I'm so tired of these Banderas. No one's ever even seen them! Have you?"

Alexander sniffed, a bit annoyed at the term. The Banderas were what people had begun calling Ukrainians fighting against the Soviet occupation. They were named for Stepan Bandera, a political activist and former leader of the first Ukrainian nationalist and independence movement, who had died in 1959.

"I don't think so," he replied.

Tatyana kicked her legs out and sprung up from her chair, where she had been idly jotting down notes on a cream-colored notebook. "Oh, I have to finish an interview, actually! Come with me. It'll be interesting."

Alexander walked to her and took both her hands in his. "On one condition: If they call me from work, we have to leave."

"Deal."

Forty minutes later, they arrived at a small house with a large and well-kept yard. The gate was open. Tatyana knocked on the door. A few minutes later, a lean, elderly man wearing a purple cardigan and khaki pants appeared at the door. He held a newspaper in one hand, and straightened his glasses with the other.

"Come in, come in," the old man said happily. They followed him into the house, which was roomier than it looked from the outside. There were a number of black and white photographs on the walls; men in uniform, staring balefully at the camera. The place seemed steeped in history.

He led them to the kitchen. "Take a seat at the table, and I'll bring some tea. My neighbor just brought me some fresh stuffed pies, so let's have tea together." He placed the paper on the table and went into the kitchen.

Alexander glanced at the newspaper. "He reads English?" he asked in disbelief.

"And not just English."

Before Tatyana could explain further, the old man returned with hot tea and a plate of fresh, fragrant pies. He placed everything on the table, and sat down. "Please, dig in."

"Valentin, let me introduce Alexander, my fiancé."

Valentin set his teacup aside, extended his hand to Alexander, and trained a long, piercing gaze at him, sizing him up. "I think you've done well, Tatyana. A good choice. An interesting man." He gazed into Alexander's eyes. "And you, sir, have not made a mistake in your choice. Jewels like Tanya are the stuff of dreams nowadays. Take good care of her."

"I promise, I will."

Valentin picked up his tea once again. He took several sips before turning to Tatyana. "So to finish our interview–"

Tatyana interrupted him. "Don't be upset with me. You either, Alex." She looked at Alexander sheepishly. "Promise me you won't."

"We promise," Alexander and Valentin said, almost in unison.

"You see, Valentin, Alex is Russian but he has never seen a live Bandera. I thought this would be a good opportunity to introduce him to one in person."

Alexander smiled thinly before shaking his head slightly. He should have known Tatyana had planned something other than a mere interview.

Valentin laughed heartily. "Remember this historic moment, Alex, because there are very few of us remaining in the world. Believe me. Thank Mr. Putin. He revived our memory only to make us disappear into oblivion. I am happy to tell our story to a man who is willing to listen."

"Valentin was telling me about the ten million Ukrainians who perished," Tatyana explained to Alex.

"It was a terrible period for the Ukrainian people," Valentin said sadly. "From 1924 to 1940, millions of people died from hunger and repression—that's one out of every five Ukrainians. Not only did our bodies suffer, but our minds as well; they closed down the newspapers and the theaters, and enforced atheism. But out of these difficult conditions, a movement emerged for Ukrainian independence. The Soviet ideologues called us *Banderas*."

Tatyana grabbed Alexander's hand in excitement. "Last time he mentioned how one member of the Secret Police saved his entire group." She turned to Valentin. "How did the Secret Police know where you were? Were you betrayed, or was it just by chance? How did you even get into the Ukrainian Insurgent Army?"

"One question at a time! I got into the UPA very simply. My cousin, Ivas, was the district leader of the UPA. He introduced me to the underground world, where my main task was gathering information on the location and movement of Soviet troops and the KGB's operations."

Valentin paused to take a sip of tea, lubricating his dry throat before resuming. "When I came across important information, I had to either deliver it to the underground headquarters myself, or stash it in a secret box. These were located in different places. Later, another messenger would take this information and deliver it to the right place. As a rule, associates didn't know each other, so if the operation failed, they couldn't give up their comrades under torture."

He pushed the plate of pies closer to Alexander. "Please, enjoy. They really are quite scrumptious."

He paused for a few moments, as if lost in his memories, before continuing his story.

"It was the eve of Soviet Army Day—and yes, someone betrayed us. We never did find out who. In one of the villages, not very far from our fortification, an operating KGB group was positioned in one of the best houses. The Reds had exiled the owner, a good-natured and hard-working farmer, to Siberia. They used his home for different administrative purposes. To lift up the villagers' national spirit, we decided to celebrate Soviet Army Day in our own way. A few days before February 23, we hid our Ukrainian flag near the KGB group's headquarters. Then the eve of February 23, six of us went to the village. The Secret Police numbered more than sixty, *so they were armed to the teeth*."

"Who supplied you with arms and ammunition?" Tatyana asked.

"Our enemies," Valentin said, smiling. "We took what we needed from them."

Tatyana and Alexander both nodded in grim understanding.

"It was a lovely evening. The frosty sky was studded with stars, the trees rustled gently, shrouded in snow. Icy snow crunched under our feet as we tried to go quietly. A small group of young women were waiting for us at the entry to the village. They knew about our plan. We needed their help to get us to the headquarters. We sang, joked, and laughed. No one suspects the happy or the drunk." Valentin winked at Tatyana.

"Once we got near the headquarters, the women began flirting with the guards. We snuck away and took our positions, armed with a pistol, a couple of grenades, and a dagger. As the women chatted with the guards, one of our brave soldiers quietly climbed onto the roof of the headquarters, took down the Soviet flag, and hoisted our Ukrainian flag in its place. He tacked a sign saying 'mined' to the flagpole. When he was done, we quietly dispersed while the women continued to joke and laugh with the guards."

Valentin paused to finish off his tea before continuing, a look of satisfaction on his face.

"The next day, around lunchtime, a huge crowd gathered at the headquarters. Everyone was staring at the roof, where the wind had unfurled the *blue and yellow* flag of Ukraine. The Secret Police were running around the building, swearing aloud."

Tatyana laughed, "Why didn't anyone try to take it down?"

"No one dared to climb onto the roof until the engineers had come and checked for explosives. And only in the evening, after they found that the roof was not in fact mined, was the Ukrainian flag removed and the Soviet flag put back." A smile spread across Valentin's face. "Supposedly several KGB officers lost their ranks, and the new commander was tasked with locating and destroying the UPA in the area as quickly as possible."

In that moment, his smile slowly began to fade.

"A few weeks later, we came back from a mission early in the morning. It was still dark out. Our hideout was under a brick barn, and the anxious voice of our hostess warned us through a vent to be careful, as several trucks of Secret Police had surrounded the farm. We had been tired, but our fatigue quickly vanished."

Valentin's voice had grown quieter, yet somehow more urgent. Alexander could sense the old man was steeling himself for the events to follow, which were clearly difficult to talk about, even so many years later.

"We discussed what to do. Soon we heard voices through the vent. The Secret Police were searching the house. If they found us, we were doomed. We had a small radio, along with a receiver, a typewriter, a lot of leaflets and literature, weapons and ammunition. But the most important documents were the names, aliases, addresses of safe places, passwords, and codes. We prepared to destroy it all. Then we heard our hostess through the vent once again. The Secret Police were surrounding our brick barn."

"Valentin, how could they find you? Was it only by the vent or there were the other ways to find your positions?" Tatyana asked.

"Not only the vents, Tanya." Valentin replied. "They had long metal rods. Step by step they jammed those rods into the ground. If our guys didn't dig deep enough, or didn't press the ground good enough, then it wasn't difficult for them to find our position. But this didn't happen often."

"You must have been terrified!" Tatyana said, gripping his hand across the small tea table.

"Fear, Tanya it is normal feeling for all people. Only you must know how to control it. At that moment, Tanya, we had no time to be afraid. And I had already seen so much death."

Valentin seemed to get lost in his memories once again, struggling to pick up the thread of his thoughts. Tatyana and Alexander sipped their tea, waiting for him to continue.

"Our commander gave us specific instructions, about what we had to do if we were detected," he said suddenly. "I was the youngest in the squad and the thinnest. The hatch opening was circular and narrow, less than one meter in diameter. As soon as the Secret Police started to open the hatch, I was to throw a bunch of grenades into the barn, then jump out of the hideout and open fire on the barn door with a machine gun, allowing the others to get out. After that, we had to rush to escape, covering each other in an attempt to break through the encirclement and escape into the woods. After our orders, we sang the Ukrainian national anthem in a whisper and took our positions."

"Being the first to jump out and cover the others—that's quite the responsibility for someone so young," Alexander said.

Valentin did not answer. He stood, and shuffled back into the kitchen. He returned with a kettle of water and refreshed the teapot. "I moved to the hatch, and began to shove the grenades and *magazines* under my coat. I was not religious, but remember whispering softly, 'Remember me, Lord, like the thief on the cross.'"

He finished pouring the water but did not sit down yet, leaning one weathered hand on the table.

"And then time stood still," he whispered. "We listened for the slightest rustle or thud. We didn't know what was going on up top—whether our hostess was alive or not, and how much longer the search would last. Minutes turned into an eternity. Eight hours passed silent as a tomb."

Alexander whistled lowly in appreciation.

"Eight hours?" Tatyana asked quietly.

The old fighter spoke up again. "Finally, our hostess came to tell us they'd left—the Secret Police were gone. But one of them had saved our lives. She explained how they had entered the house, and crawled around everywhere—under the bed, under the tables, rearranging things—searching for a hatch. Then one of them swore and grabbed his leg. She had given him a stool, which he placed right on top of our vent. He'd spent quite a bit of time checking his foot, unwrapping old bandages, searching for new injury. In fact, he continued that the whole time they searched the house. When they moved on, he'd stayed behind and warned the hostess to tell us to get out, that we'd been betrayed."

"So you escaped unharmed," Tatyana said, leaning back in her chair in relief. "But another time you were wounded and captured, right?"

He nodded as he took a few more sips of tea. "Once, my bodyguard—as we would call him today—and I had to pick up passports for our group so we could go to the south of the Soviet Union, to Russian Georgia, and legally work there. The Soviet Army colonel was waiting for us. He was our guy. With his help we were to get inside of the Soviet military. Our main targets were the Soviet propaganda and Soviet Secret Services."

"How many people were in your group?" Alexander asked around a mouthful of pie.

"Six, with me as the leader. Unfortunately, nothing worked out. We found the right address. My team trained their guns on the doors while I walked around the side of house to knock on a window. Instead of the expected answer, I heard a crash, followed by a few short rounds of gunfire and then someone yelling 'ambush!'

"From the erupting gunfire and rockets, the night became as bright as day." Valentin sighed and shook his head, idly twisting a fork in his hand.

"The KGB had been waiting for us. Somehow, we managed to escape through the gardens and began retreating into the forest." He offered a knowing smile to his guests. "The KGB wouldn't go into the forest; they were afraid of our forests. We were nearly there when a stray bullet got lodged in the magazine of my machine gun. My machine gun jammed. And just then I felt a dull thrust to my leg, followed by another in my stomach. I fell, clutching my stomach. Hot blood was everywhere. I reached for my holster, but the gun was gone. Lost."

"Did you think you could shoot your way out?" Tatyana asked nervously.

Valentin and Alexander shared a sympathetic look.

"No, my dear. I didn't want to be captured alive."

"Several Russian officers and soldiers surrounded me. One officer raised his machine gun, pointed it at me and said, 'Now son of a bitch, I will make a screen out of you'. But another officer stopped him, saying I could still be useful to them. He gave the command to put me into the truck. I passed out after that."

"But you survived," Tatyana pointed out.

"Yes, I survived. They began questioning me as soon as I came to my senses. I never gave up anyone's name," he said through gritted teeth. "All that I knew and everyone that I knew remained with me, no matter what they did. They called a doctor and told him to start doing surgery on me. They told him not to worry much about my life. I am not sure the day, but one or two days after surgery, the same officer who saved my life came into my room with a cup of wine. Nobody was in the room."

"Drink," he said. "You lost a lot of blood and you need to get your strength back."

Tatyana leaned forward. This was a part of the story she hadn't heard. "But who was it?" she asked. "Who would have risked such a thing?"

"I don't know who he was. He never told me, and I never asked him. I just know one thing: he saved my life. As soon as I could stand, and when they had tired of trying to wring information out of me, they took me to prison. Death row. I had a cell to myself. No bed, no chair, no window. I slept half-sitting on the concrete floor. No one survived there long."

Valentin sank into thought.

"You know, even in the most hellish of places, like that cell, there are moments when I believed in the spirit of humanity. That our brotherly love would, somehow, even in the face of so much destruction, triumph." He smiled, wistfully.

Tatyana and Alexander remained silent, waiting for him to continue.

Valentin picked at one of the pies but did not eat it. "I don't know how much time passed, but eventually three officers arrived—Troika, we called them—to read out my verdict. I was originally to be sentenced to the highest measure of punishment…by firing squad. After an excruciatingly long pause, a colonel read that the death sentence had been commuted to twenty-five years in Ozlagerey, a special labor camp closed from the world."

"He did that on purpose, didn't he—the pause?" Tatyana asked.

"Maybe so. I remember my life passing before my eyes; Ukraine, Germany, Czechia, and Poland. I could see and feel these places, places I thought I would never see again. I was still so young, but I had already followed so many roads.

"The only thing I couldn't see was the future. I still had to go through it, and all of these adventures began from that death row cell. To the far north with its polar nights and permafrost, and from there to the sultry deserts and steppes of Kazakhstan. Sometimes, I still feel nauseous from what I witnessed and experienced in those God-forsaken Soviet camps. It's hard to believe that a single man could have gone through all of this, get to the Crimean peninsula, to the shores of the Black Sea, and still stay alive. I thought all of this would never happen again, but I was mistaken."

Valentin paused for a moment, as if trying to reorient himself to the present. Then he gently took Tatyana's hand.

"As you can see, Tatyana, sometimes life takes us along a razor's edge, but we have to be able to keep our balance even in the most critical situations. Now you must *promise* me that you will not lose your way."

"I'll try not to."

"Don't *try*, Tanechka. *Do*."

"I promise, I won't lose my way."

Valentin picked up his unfinished glass of tea, slowly raised it to his lips, and just as slowly looked up at Alexander. Their eyes met. Neither dropped his gaze. Valentin set the teacup down without drinking. "You are an officer of the Russian army."

Alexander smiled enigmatically. "Yes."

"Don't be offended, and don't hide your anger. Maybe you didn't like hearing this story, but I have only told you the truth—all of it. But what is happening today, I don't understand it. Is the cycle repeating or simply continuing where we left it so many decades ago…" Valentin's voice trailed off.

"I neither resent you nor feel angry," Alexander assured the old man. "I am sincerely grateful. Stories like these enrich our lives, and sometimes help us to see the other side of the coin."

His phone vibrated loudly on the table. Alexander glanced at the number, but did not take the call. He looked up at Valentin and Tatyana. "Would you please excuse me? I have to return this. I'll just step outside?"

"Tatyana and I will be here. We'll wait for you."

Alexander quietly slipped out a side door, into a small, pleasant garden. After a few short words and nods, he hung up. A moment later, he stepped back inside.

"Excuse us, Valentin. It was a call from my work and we have to go."

"So, you're saying this call was a call from your work and not from your duty station?" Valentin asked with a grin.

This took Alexander by surprise. He may have been out of the game for a while, but Valentin still new how to play. It would be enough for the Bandera to hear just one wrong word for Alexander to be revealed as a special worker. "To carry out my duty," answered Alexander with a smile.

They shared a knowing laugh as Tatyana looked from one to the other in disbelief and confusion.

Before they left, Valentin gave Tatyana a few pages of old, crumpled documents, obviously kept in hiding for a long period of time. Tatyana looked at the first line, "We didn't shoot them, we just killed them like this, with the butt." Tatyana was at a loss and looked at Valentin with a flash of horror. "What is this?"

"Read it through, Tatyana, and you'll understand. This is real life."

They said their goodbyes, and Alexander and Tatyana got back into the car. As they drove back to Sevastopol, Tatyana read the document aloud.

"I heard the story of this brave woman from one of the sadistic murderers of the 1940s, Ivano-Frankivsk, at the Stanislavsky prison. I met him in the former USSR, in Zheleznovodsk, one of the sanatoriums. I don't remember the exact name of this woman, but I believe that eventually the secret KGB documents will become public and we will find out the name of the heroine who fought in the units of the Ukrainian Insurgent Army. My conscience and honor will not allow me to be silent about this hero and the atrocities committed by the KGB agents.

My roommate in the sanatorium was constantly intoxicated, but especially so in the afternoons. Then he would get in bed without undressing and snore. Something about him resembled a petulant pig. He was not that old, in his fifties. I should add that this was in the sixties. However, alcohol had ruined his looks, and he appeared much older. He often got angry, so I didn't want to drink with him.

To that he said, 'So, do you know who I am? Soviet army generals regarded me well, and you don't entertain drinking with me?'

After a while, almost dead drunk, he bared his dirty soul. 'Do you know why I drink?'

'No, I don't.'

'I keep seeing the people I killed.'

'And you didn't get prosecuted for it?'

'No. I fulfilled my duty to my country, the government, and the Communist Party. First, I learned to kill in the mine-laying battalion around Stalingrad. There I had to kill all sorts of people, both theirs and ours. The truth is, shooting our own was pitiful, but the others weren't a big deal. When I was in Stanislav, they brought many Banderas to us in prison. I did not feel sorry for killing them. But then a female Bandera walked into my life, and to this day I can't forget her.

'Long story short, they said that she had kept shooting to her last cartridge. She put down a platoon of our soldiers. She tried to blow herself up with a grenade, but the grenade misfired. They took her alive. She was a priest's daughter, twenty-two years old. She was an operative in the UPA. Even with all of my hatred for the Banderas, I was taken by her light blue eyes, beautiful tender face, lush curls of black hair, elegant waist, and leather jacket and boots. This was how I remember her when she was brought in for questioning—before we started to torture her.

Her courage and boldness only incited more vile anger and hatred in those who interrogated her. She knew that she would be killed. She didn't give up anyone. What didn't we do to her? We tortured her endlessly. First, we beat her with phone cord whips, then put her fingers in a door and pushed so hard that the skin on her fingers split. We tore the nails from her toes, hung her by her hair, pricked her breasts, hung her by her feet. She fell unconscious several times, and when she did we poured water on her and started over. When she came to, she stood up and, instead of answering our questions, spat blood in our faces.

The bitch Bandera gave up no one. And, to boot, during one of the interrogations, she grabbed the decanter that stood on a table and smashed it against the investigator's head. After that, they only brought her in for interrogation in handcuffs. But that didn't last long. The Troika handed down her death sentence and I was the one to carry out the execution. At that time, we were killing about ten people a day. In order to do work like that, I usually drank about a pint of vodka before. It was easier to kill that way, a little tipsy. All the same, I was killing humans.'

'And no one asked for reprieve?'

'In my experience, there was none of that. Beaten, broken, and shattered, they went crossing themselves, or saying prayers, and they still shouted *Glory to Ukraine*...but didn't ask for anything more. Generally, they were not told that they were about to die, they just felt it.'

'You frequently say *we* killed them, or *I* killed them. What do you mean, you shot them?'

'No. We didn't put them against a wall. We did it with the hammer we used to pound on train cars. And it was very simple, almost bloodless. You know, you lead a man down the corridor until a certain place, pull out the hammer hidden in the sleeve of your jacket, and hit them as hard as you can on the back of the head, on the crown. The body would jerk a few times, and that was it. But, let me tell you, it was dignified, we didn't have to waste ammo and there was almost no blood.'

My cellmate spoke so enthusiastically and with such repulsive passion. Not a nerve moved on his face. Not a drop of regret or remorse—psychopathy kept alive by the cheap vodka made in sanitarium toilets.

'You know, just before killing this bitch Bandera, all three of us wanted to rape her. She lunged, the scum, as best she could. She bit the others and me but didn't give up. When I led her down the corridor, she realized that she was going to die, and shouted, 'Farewell, brothers, Dzvinka is going to die,' then she turned to me and said something with hatred and started singing.'

'What did she sing?'

'Imagine, after all these horrors, after all those tortures, she sang the Bandera anthem...she told me that Ukraine had not yet died.'

'And then what?'

'What next? As soon as she stood on the sewer grate, I took the hammer out of my sleeve and hit her hard on the head, but I missed a little. I was pretty drunk. And the bitch first dropped to her knees then on her hands, but not down on the grate. So I pressed my foot on her, pushing her into the sewer grate, and began to smack her with the hammer 'till her brains spilled out.'

'And then…?'

'Nothing, she jerked a few times and that was it. I wiped the blood and brains off my boots. When I flipped her to take off the handcuffs, I saw that her eyes were open. They were looking right at me. Until this day, I see those eyes.'

'And your conscience doesn't torment you?'

'What conscience? Was I the only one who did it? No, all we did was walk away afterward, get good and drunk, and it's conscionable. You think it was for nothing that the Captain gave me a prize, on top of all the other awards I received? How many did I kill? There's no counting. Sometimes, though, I have nightmares, and that woman never leaves me. All these years she haunts me, the middle part of the day is worst, when I am awake and the memories come too easily. Sometimes, I go down the hall and it feels like she's walking with me. I turn around but no one is there. I go on and she's with me again. Tell me, how do I get rid of her?'

Hardly finishing those last words, the drunk sadist fell into his bed without undressing—another day spent so pitifully."

Tatyana brushed away a tear with her palm, and then looked questioningly at Alexander. "Is this true? We were taught the opposite in school—that we defended ourselves honorably, that all the others were bastards."

"I don't know," Alexander replied in a cold metallic voice. After a few seconds, in a softer voice he added, "I understand your feelings, but right now I see it all only as information. Purely professional. I was raised in another world. Maybe we should talk about this tomorrow."

CHAPTER 6

About an hour and a half later, they arrived at Alexander's apartment building. Alexander jumped out of the car and opened the door for Tatyana. He got her bag, laptop, and camera from the trunk. He hugged her, kissed her, and softly whispered in her ear, "Don't get upset with me. Just wait for me and I'll be back." Then he got back in the car and disappeared into the twilight of the fleeing day, leaving her still a bit shaken by the document she had just read.

Tatyana entered the sparsely decorated apartment. It was small, but neat. Nothing was extra. The bookcase held photographs between the books. Searching reflexively for some comfort, Tatyana pulled a few of photos from between the pages and smiled. She and Alexander were in each of them: Yalta, Odessa, St. Sophia's Cathedral in Kiev, St. Basil's Cathedral in Moscow, and Peterhof in Saint Petersburg. Memories emerged, replacing the terrible images that had been in her mind.

Finally, she walked to the television and turned on the news. All channels showed the same: armored personnel carriers, cars, soldiers, and hundreds of posters on homes and fences proclaiming "Crimea—Russian land. Crimea is ours, fellow Russians! Down with the Banderas and those who associate with them." One Ukrainian channel mentioned something about plans for an assault on the Belbek Airfield, but it cut out abruptly. Tatyana did not change the channel. What if it came back on again?

She pulled her laptop from her bag, set it on her lap, and started working, hoping the clip would come back on. She kicked off her shoes and settled into the couch, watching the developments unfold and keeping an eye on both the television and her computer. Several hours later, fatigue from the day's activities caught up with her and she stretched out her legs. Within minutes, she was deeply asleep.

In her sleep, it seemed to her that she heard a conversation in Ukrainian. It felt like a dream, but her natural curiosity slowly woke her. She opened her eyes, and on the screen, a Ukrainian commentator was pointing towards a gate where soldiers and armored personnel carriers were headed. The assault on Belbek Airfield was imminent, and according to the correspondent, it could turn into a huge armed battle at any moment.

Tatyana scrambled to her feet, grabbed her phone and camera, and ran out the front door and down the driveway. She glanced up and down the street, but there wasn't a single taxi. *Just what I need*, she thought. Finally, she was able to get the attention of a Georgian driver who agreed to give her a ride to Belbek.

"It's dangerous to be headed to the airfield now," the driver said as he sped through nearly empty streets. "And a dangerous place for a woman. Full of Russian bastards and tanks—oh excuse me, are you Russian or Ukrainian?"

"Ukrainian. I'm a journalist."

"I thought so. A beautiful woman like you can only be Ukrainian." He was quiet for a few minutes. "I used to live in the Caucasus, but when the Russians came and started a war where we lived, I ran away from them to come here, to Crimea. Now they even came here with their war." He slowed the car as they neared the airfield. "Please, be careful. Don't trust them."

Tatyana rifled through her pockets, and held out money for him. He refused to take it.

"I will not take it from you. Just write the truth. For my sake. We need voices like yours." He smiled sadly.

Tatyana took a deep breath and smiled to him. "I will," she said. She exited the car and walked toward the airfield.

Alexander was at a small mud hut, built long before the war, on the outskirts of the city. He was fifteen minutes late. A guard stopped him at the entrance, and Alexander flashed his identification. The guard glanced at it with mild disinterest, then reported the visitor through the radio. There was a crackle on the other end.

"Let him through," said an unfamiliar voice.

Alexander entered a large room with dim lighting. There were some electric lanterns, giving off just enough light that he could make out what looked like a war room. Several officers in camouflage uniforms were sitting at a small round table, sidearms visible. The general, also in camouflage, was seated in front of the door. He introduced Alexander to the officers, who were SWAT.

"You'll lead the team to capture the airfield," the General said. "Provoke the Ukrainians to open fire first. Not just a few shots. A whole company, or at least a platoon, must open fire. It'd be desirable to set up the civilians. Just remember that the area is teeming with Western intelligence agencies and special reporters. Your every step and action will be monitored." The General frowned to emphasize his point. "The West is already trying to pressure us. If the situation does not go according to plan, turn around. Just get out, we can't afford for this to go wrong. Then try to organize talks and do everything you can to make the Ukrainians cross over to our side. I don't care what you promise them. Report the results to me and me alone. Any questions?"

There were none, and the General left.

Soon the men were arguing the points among themselves. Two Russian commandos argued that they should at least ask the Ukrainians to surrender first. Two Chechens, clearly well-versed in the chain of command, were quick to react, pointing out that the Russians were intentionally ignoring the General's plans. One of them threatened to report this to the General immediately, to which one of the Russians growled that he'd rather waste a bullet on him than on a Ukrainian. The Chechens broke out into a loud argument and stepped into the yard to discuss amongst themselves. The other Russian turned to Alexander and asked why he had remained silent.

"I'm listening to you guys." After a pause, he added, "We can come to them secretly at night, visit them, and talk to the officers. We know that most of them have been living in communes with their families. These are a hopeless lot; they have had no future for the last two decades. We have a real opportunity to offer them titles, positions, and—most importantly—apartments for their families. Does this option work for you?"

The others glanced at one another. There was very little fight in them, it seemed, now that the Chechens had left. They agreed. Alexander nodded. "Good. But tell me," he went on, "what led you to such a peaceful solution to this problem so quickly? After all, you *did* directly violate the orders of the general. What stands behind your decision?"

The taller of the two Russians looked meaningfully at his compatriot, clearly questioning how to respond. A few seconds later, a look of resolve washed over his face. He set his strong jaw and explained:

"A few weeks ago, I received an order to disarm a Coast Guard contingent with a small group of our Special Forces. Previous efforts had not ended with peace talks, and I was ordered to break into their area and disarm 'Ukropov' with as little fuss as possible. I ordered the driver of the BTR to break through the gates of the property at full speed. At the last moment, when the gate was just meters away, out stepped a Ukrainian, with an RPG in one hand and a gun in the other." He looked at his fellow Russian, who nodded for him to continue.

The tall Russian sighed. "My emotions got the better of me and I screamed at the driver to stop. I was not thinking about the repercussions; I had recognized him. His name is Mikola. I jumped out of the vehicle and ran to him. He saw me and, in joy and surprise, threw his weapons to the ground, opened his arms, and hugged me. Those around us cheered us on."

"Some shouted that it was a disgrace, Peter," the other man interjected.

Peter crossed his arms. "Mikola asked why I was there. I told him I was following orders. He told us to ignore those orders and to get out of there. He asked why we were shooting each other for the sake of 'those Kremlin bastards.'" Peter shrugged. "At that moment, I couldn't have cared less about my military career. I gave the order to move away."

"And your superiors?" Alexander asked.

"I lied, and told them that there had been many civilians and some international reporters present. That the situation was too hot, and that we had to get out. I don't know if they believed me or not, but at least they pretended to believe me." He put an arm around his friend's shoulders, who appeared somewhat uncomfortable.

"When Victor and I were in Chechnya, we were in the same squad. We were ordered to break through a canyon to get to Grozny, but we were ambushed. In the canyon, the Chechens simply burned everyone. A man named Mikola—yes, the very same—saved us, pulling Victor and I from a burning armored personnel carrier. I had a broken leg and my back was badly burned. Victor broke his arm, fractured his hip, and had burns all over—you see the scars on his head. Victor and I practically had no chance of survival and we didn't want to end up in the hands of the Chechens, but Mikola persuaded us to save our strength. The next day, he made a sled out of tree branches, piled Vic and I on it, harnessed himself like a horse, and dragged us away." He shook his head, smiling slightly as he reflexively held Victor's shoulder a little tighter.

"We didn't start this war," Victor spat, shrugging away Peter's arm. "The Kremlin fooled us with Chechnya then. We believed them when they told us that Chechens are terrorists at night who blow up apartment buildings while everyone is sleeping. All the secret work of the FSB." He spat dryly again, his agitation increasing. "They manipulated our feelings of patriotism. How many of our own were killed—and the Chechens? All trying to prove how patriotic we were."

"And now it's Banderas or fascists or who-the-hell else instead of Chechens," Peter continued. "They've even thrown Kadyrov's Chechens into the fight against the Banderas and the fascists. Have you ever seen a bandera or fascist anywhere? I only see guys with whom—just yesterday—we played cards or ate and drank well with. Yesterday they were our brothers. Today the Kremlin idiots have labeled them Banderas and Nazis. They lied to us about Chechnya. This won't happen with Ukraine."

"And Mikola?" Alexander asked.

"When I hugged him, I whispered in his ear that three hundred meters to the west, a platoon of the bearded Kadyrov's men were ready to attack at any moment. He hugged me tighter and said they'd finish shaving those bastards. So to answer your question... after all we've been through, I'd rather have my hands wither away than direct the muzzle of a machine gun toward another Mikola."

Alexander was touched by this, but he kept his feelings well hidden. His training had allowed him to play any role, and he knew that even if Peter and Victor were telling the truth, the Chechens outside were a whole other matter. Still, the young Russians' story had affected him, and he thought about Tatyana. The most sacred moments of their lives flashed through his mind. A sharp voice interrupted his thoughts, as the Chechens, clearly out of patience, came barging back in.

"Has our commander made a decision?" The Chechen's voice was only slightly antagonistic.

"Yes, he has," Alexander answered calmly. "No provocation. Not one shot. Understood?"

"Yes, commander."

"A soft commander, you are," one of the Chechens said sarcastically.

"That's not for you to decide," said Alexander, but he was equally surprised by what he was doing.

The next morning at 10:30, Alexander and his team drove up to the gates of the airfield. He hadn't slept well. His dreams were a strange mixture of the stories from Valentin and Peter, with Tatyana getting lost inside giant teacups and an overwhelming sense of dread. All he really cared about in those dreams was where she was. He was up well before dawn, and watched the sky turn from slate to gray to orange as the sun rose.

Soon, they were approaching their destination. He stopped the armored vehicles about fifty meters from the gate. He put on his mask and headed towards the gate with Peter and Victor. The morning air was clear. Marines blocked their way.

"I am Lieutenant Colonel Ivanov," Alexander called out. "I need to speak to the commander of this unit."

"Hand over your weapons," growled one of the marines.

Alexander handed over his pistol and machine gun. Peter and Victor followed suit, though they both made clear from their body language that it was a hard thing to do. The marines opened the gates. "Wait here," one of them said. "We'll call the commander." Within ten minutes, a slender, broad-shouldered Colonel approached them in full uniform.

Alexander introduced himself and his men. The Colonel was unimpressed, and highly suspicious.

"Take off your mask and show me your documents," he said.

As Alexander did so, he was startled by a familiar voice.

"What the hell are you doing in Ukrainian territory? Get your tanks the hell out of here!"

"Sorry, Colonel," he said as pulled his mask back on. He turned, and that was when he noticed a large crowd of journalists with cameras had begun to gather next to the gate. At first, he thought nothing of it, and then his eyes alighted on a familiar shock of light brown hair above an impetuous, pretty face. Tatyana stood in the first row, her camera in her hands.

Alexander's heart fluttered in his chest, and he firmly pulled Peter and Victor aside. He pointed out Tatyana to them. "You see that woman? Take her to the bus station and put her on the bus to Yalta. Intimidate her with something. Make up some kind of horror story on the way there if you have to, but do not harm her in any way. Just get her to Yalta safe and sound. This is not an order. This is a personal request."

Peter and Victor nodded and bounded toward the gate as Alexander turned back to the Colonel. They exchanged IDs, but the Colonel barely looked at Alexander's document. His attention was on a commotion developing at the gate. Alexander turned and smiled as he saw Peter pick up Tatyana and carry her over his shoulder to the NAMVI. She was smacking him on the head and on his back while Victor, two machine guns slung over his shoulder, hopelessly tried to calm her down. "Who do you think you are?!" she yelled ferociously but ineffectively, trying to escape her captors.

The Colonel noticed Alexander's smile, and when Alexander turned back to him, gave him a questioning look.

"A small personal issue," Alexander explained.

"It's bad when the affairs of the state overlap with your personal life."

"I agree." Alexander took a deep breath. "Shall we get to it? I have two options. You can either willingly hand over the airfield, or I take it by force."

The Colonel eyed him for a moment, as if sizing him up. Alexander was not fooled by the ploy, meant to make him feel uneasy. Finally, the Colonel spoke.

"Let's not rush our negotiations. I have arrested five of your men. They have achieved some degree of success, convincing ten of our soldiers and one officer to cross to your side. Don't worry, we won't shoot them."

"What do you plan on doing with them?" Alexander asked.

"Give them to you. Take your own and the traitors. Someday they'll betray you too." The Colonel snickered quietly. "Just understand one thing: You don't have enough apartments or job positions for all of us. When you run out of gifts to give, you can no longer buy our loyalty."

"Your resources are already strained, Colonel. That's no secret. Most of your planes can't even take off."

The Colonel nodded slowly. "That's true. But don't underestimate the power of oaths and duty to the motherland. We didn't come to your territory as occupiers; you came to ours. If just one of your tanks or armed soldiers crosses over to our territory, they'll be destroyed. Have no doubt about it. I will defend this base until the last bullet. If Kiev gives the order to leave the base, I will be the last to leave. I will get the time Kiev needs to deal with this issue. I think you understand that our actions are decided by Kiev and Moscow. We are merely implementers of their will."

"Speaking frankly, Colonel, I too prefer a peaceful path. However, I know that there are people who are eager for blood."

"I will give the order right now and your goods will be brought out to the gate."

"Thank you, Colonel. We'll stop here for now."

Alexander returned to his apartment late in the evening. When he turned on his cell phone, he found almost a dozen missed calls from Tatyana. He called her back, but before he could say a word after she answered, she peppered him with questions—was he okay, was he hurt, why hadn't he been answering her calls?

"Everything's okay," he said, trying to sound as reassuring as he could through the barrage of breathless questions. "You know I have to turn off my phone sometimes."

Satisfied that he was all right, she launched into a description of her day at the airfield. "Three of your guys—some Russian morons—came onto the territory of the Ukrainian military unit to talk to some Ukrainian officer. I think that it was their commander. Before I knew it, two walked over to the gate and one of them—without a single word of warning—slung me over his shoulder and carried me to a military car!"

"Did they offend you in some way?" Alexander asked, feigning shock and concern.

"Actually, no." She paused, looking thoughtful. "And I was smacking him on the head, which was obviously as hard as rock. I'm surprised I didn't break my own hand. They took me to the bus station and put me on the bus. They even paid for my ticket! But then one of them pointed a gun at the bus driver's head while the other one leveled a machine gun at the passengers and said that if I got off the bus before Yalta, all of them would be shot. Then one of them asked me if I understood that the fate of all these passengers was in my hands." Tatyana's voice quivered.

"And what did you answer them?" He had to hand it to Peter and Victor; they had done the job well, and with more creativity than he would have thought.

On the other end of the line, Tatyana stiffened and gained a look of complete control, squinting her eyes in a threatening manner. "That they should get the hell out of there and the faster they did, the better," she said resolutely.

Alexander nodded, keeping his face serious. He was happy that she couldn't see him shaking with silent laughter.

CHAPTER 7

"The events in Ukraine are not necessarily developing in our favor," the General Trofimov informed Alexander over the phone. "A full-scale operation to capture the southwestern part of Ukraine failed. Our leaders underestimated the reaction of NATO and the United States."

Alexander nodded at the phone. The General's frustration was apparent in his voice. "The situation in the world is unpredictable," he said in an attempt to diffuse the tension.

The General grunted. "Before your upcoming trip to the United States, we need for you to take part in combat operations. This experience may come in handy on that side of the ocean. Donetsk first, in the next two or three days. Be ready. This business trip won't be long. Moscow needs you in the United States more than in Donetsk."

"And my cover during this trip to America?"

"You'll go there as a journalist."

Alexander's mouth went dry. He cleared his throat several times before speaking again. "Comrade General, what kind of journalist can you make out of me?"

The General scoffed. "It doesn't matter. We'll sacrifice a few of our oligarchs and make your articles the most interesting and popular. All of America and Western Europe will be talking about them. The material will be juicy and intriguing."

He was growing increasingly more confident in the plan, and went on, "Dozens of the world's radio and television companies and other media sources will want to meet with you. You are to recruit the most popular hosts of these companies, especially those with access to government circles and strategic and scientific centers. We are not able to compete with the West economically or militarily. Hell, NATO alone exceeds our military power by almost four times, and don't even get me started on their damned sanctions. We can't apply the same method for a hybrid war in the West as in Ukraine."

Alexander paid close attention, following the twists and turns of the General's argument. This was turning into quite the plan.

"We need to develop different, non-standard methods," the General continued, "taking into account our strengths and weaknesses. And no one in the West, not even the United States, is able to compete with us in the field of propaganda. We will win the hearts and minds of the Western public. It's only a matter of time.

They will be ours, zombies all of them, and we won't need any atomic bombs or missiles. With their own hands, we'll be able to expand the Russian Empire into America and into Western Europe."

Alexander wished he felt half as confident as the General sounded.

"One small personal question," he said. "If I'm not mistaken, your fiancée is a journalist, right?"

"For *The Crimean News*."

"Is she in Yalta right now?"

"No, she's on a business trip in Kiev."

"Sounds like you have the perfect set-up, then. We can turn to her for some help. Surely, she will take up the theme of oligarchs, and we can give her plenty of material. Maybe she can help you master your new job role—or even write the articles on your behalf. Think about it."

Alexander hung up the phone, uneasy about this turn of events. It was bad enough having to keep secrets from Tatyana, but now he was expected to use her for his own professional benefit. He would have to think long and hard about how to deal with this on his way to Donetsk.

Donetsk

Alexander arrived in Donetsk at night, along with a shipment of Russian humanitarian aid. At least, "humanitarian aid" was what the trip manifest claimed was in the packages. In reality, it was a shipment of weapons, ammunition, and fuel for the tanks. The trucks would drop off the "aid," and no one would be the wiser. On the way back, the convoy took with it the Russian wounded and deceased.

The apocalyptic scenery of Donetsk did not make him happy. In the distance, he could make out the ruins of apartment buildings in the dim moonlight. Houses, cars, and military equipment were still burning in some places. He wished, momentarily, that he could have arrived during the day, when things might have seemed a little less foreboding. The city seemed completely devoid of life, with only suffocating fumes and sepulchral silence.

His driver continued into an area on the outskirts of Donetsk and stopped near a small church with a broken dome. The paint was peeling off of the walls and at least one window had been hastily patched back together, setting the church in sharp contrast to the large and undamaged houses across the way.

"The headquarters of the checkpoint is over there." The driver pointed to a house in the middle of the block.

Alexander exited the car. Before he could make it up the front steps, the door of the house opened, and three men in camouflage uniforms came out to meet him. Their uniforms had no identifying markings. From the air about them and the way they carried themselves, it was clear that they were SWAT. A man Alexander assumed to be the Captain stepped forward to verify his documents.

Satisfied by the papers, the Captain ushered him inside. "We're here only for a few minutes, to meet you and update you about the situation. Five systems of volley fire are located in the town. All of them are positioned on the estates of town residents. This prevents return fire. The Ukrainians are aware of their coordinates, but do not shoot at their own. The minute they do, our media begins a live broadcast about Ukrainians shooting their own. We have our people working at the facilities—led by Captain Zhiltsov, you have heard of him."

The Captain handed Alexander a sealed envelope. "A specialist in sabotage activities from Moscow is arriving any day now. All of his information is in this envelope. Your sabotage group is made up of professionals. They've been through it all. Nothing is sacred for them."

The men gathered their gear.

"Please, you can make yourself comfortable," the Captain said. "The soldiers will return in an hour or two. They are on a mission right now." With that, he and his men shuffled out of the house, loaded up their gear, and disappeared into the darkness of Donetsk.

Several hours passed. Alexander poked around the house, but didn't find anything of interest. Some old food, a few books, pots and pans and towels. The sun had already risen, but nobody showed up. Every once in a while, he could hear the very distant sound of gunfire. At least, he thought that is what he heard.

Towards the evening, Alexander found himself staring out the window at the lifeless streets. *What have I gotten myself into?* he thought.

Three children—two girls with tangled hair and a smaller boy—suddenly raced out from a neighboring house, laughing and chasing each other. In the otherwise shattered landscape, it was a momentary reprieve from the anxiety and oppression Alexander felt. He smiled, remembering his own childhood. He had grown up happy, with a mother and father who loved him, far from military intrigue in Khanty-Mansiysk. It had been cold, but he remembered dancing in the street with friends when he was their age. Just as quickly, through the curtains, he watched the children run into a small shed, where a volley fire system poked out from behind one corner.

The back door to the house crashed opened, startling Alexander. A group of hardened soldiers tumbled into the living room where he was standing.

"They sent us a new one!" a man with a shaved head grumbled around the cigar in his teeth. He shoved a gun barrel into Alexander's chest and blew smoke into his face. "Well, rookie, shall we introduce ourselves?"

"All right," Alexander replied coldly, never taking his eyes from the man. "Let's get acquainted."

"Well?" He pushed the gun against Alexander's chest. "What's your damn name?"

"Alexander. And yours?"

"Demon. You like it?" He smiled, showing off darkened teeth.

Alexander didn't answer, and let his eyes wander to the other soldiers. He stopped on one standing nearby. "And yours?"

"Serpent," the man answered. He was tall and thin, with an angular face that, Alexander had to admit, did make him look a bit like a snake.

Alexander cleared his throat and pushed the barrel of Demon's gun away from his chest. He stood and approached each of the soldiers, asking their names. Boa, Vampire, Scrag. It was like a collection of horror movies. Then he noticed a very young soldier standing in the kitchen, trying to go unnoticed. Alexander walked up to him, and stuck out his hand in greeting. "What's your name, fighter?"

"Student," the boy said.

Caught by surprise, Alexander smiled right away. "You actually a student?"

Student nodded. "Third year. Majoring in law. At St. Petersburg University."

Alexander motioned toward the windows. "How did you end up here?"

"I took an academic leave to help our brotherly nation get rid of the Banderas and fascists."

"And your parents just let you go?"

"It's just my mother and two sisters." Student lowered his voice, in case they might hear from hundreds of miles away. "They don't know I'm here."

"How long you been here?"

"Three months."

Alexander nodded slowly, thinking for a moment. Then he turned and snatched a gun from one of the rebels and dropped it loudly on the table. The brotherhood looked in his direction, clearly perplexed.

"From this point on I am your commander," Alexander said forcefully. "I do not ask for your love or favor. You can hate me, but not my orders. I don't advise you to test my words."

"And what do we call you, newbie?" Demon asked sarcastically.

"For now, you can call me Alex."

"Well, Alex," Demon said, stressing the name. "I am the locomotive that moves this train. These boys, they only listen to my orders—"

Alexander cut him off. "You gave the orders until I came. Do not make me repeat myself." Demon glared at him, and Alexander met his eyes, unflinching.

Demon shrugged dismissively. "All right, lads. Let's get to the bunks. Tomorrow we have an important day," he said, clearly not wanting to hand over his authority in any way.

Alexander remained next to the window. Throughout the house, he could hear the raucous sounds of these men and smell the smoke of their hand-rolled cigarettes.

Alexander struggled to wake up the next morning. When he could finally open his eyes, Student was standing over him. Sunshine streamed through the window. How long had he slept? He jammed his hand under the pillow he had laid on the floor. The pistol and envelope were still in their place. "Where is everyone?" His voice was hoarse and cracking.

"They left me to protect you."

Alexander sat up and his head swam. "What did they give me?"

Student shrugged. "Something to smell after you fell asleep. Please don't tell them that I woke you. I was just supposed to guard you and not let anyone in."

"Did you wake me up?"

Student shrugged again.

Alexander sighed in exasperation. "I am a Russian officer with a not-so-trivial ranking. Try using your words."

"I've seen all kinds of officers—lieutenant colonels, colonels, and even generals—who came here for their orders."

"What orders?"

"The ones that Demon and the others fulfill. Jewelry, money, cars—mostly foreign cars."

Alexander squinted up at him, the sunlight making his head throb. "Where do they get them?"

"Different cities and villages. They take things with the pretext that they are needed in order to defeat Banderas and fascists. At first, people did not give up their things, but Demon organized public executions. Now everyone knows them as the 'Special Brotherhood of Russia.' They don't submit to anyone here. Someone commands them from Russia."

"What's your real name?"

"Oleg. Oleg Tarasov."

Alexander rubbed the back of his neck. "Is this what you signed up for?"

Oleg sat hunched in a chair, his face slack and pale. "It never occurred to me that I'd have to fight in this kind of army. After all, I sacrificed the university, my mother and sisters, in order to help people escape from the Banderas and the fascists who rob and kill the defenseless, peaceful population of Ukraine." He shook his head. "I can't forgive myself for being so naive."

Alexander studied the boy for a moment, the defeat obvious in his sagging shoulders. "If you no longer believe in the integrity of a Russian officer, then I swear by my mother's honor that you can trust me and rely on me. Just remember one thing: Your tongue is your enemy."

"Yes, comrade. I swear by my mother that I will keep my tongue to myself."

Alexander searched the boy's face. He was scared and confused, but seemed honest. He stuck out his hand, still prone on the bed. They exchanged a warm handshake.

Alexander got down to business. "Now try to figure out where the lads could be. Last night they said that they have a big day today. Does that tell you anything?"

Oleg scratched his head. "I can't even guess where they could be."

"Come on, Oleg, try to remember what they were talking about, where they were, and what they were doing just before they left. You're a future lawyer, right? This isn't a theoretical exam. These are your skills and talents in practical life."

Oleg stared out the window. "I try not to listen to them too closely. Two weeks ago, they shot through the crowd at a small Protestant church during a Sunday service, just to take two foreign cars."

"Were its members armed? Did they show resistance?"

"No. Just refused to swear allegiance to the Russian Orthodox Church. None of the Protestants came out of the church." Oleg turned to look at Alexander, the pain heavy in his eyes. "There were children there as well."

"What happened?"

"Our media was called. And they broadcast live about the atrocities that the Banderas and Ukrainian fascists had just committed, sponsored by the Americans. Our Special Forces had arrived just minutes too late to save the victims and their children. No mention about the missing foreign cars."

"Where are they?"

"They were here, behind the house." Oleg motioned toward the far end of the house. "There's a tent garage. Then four people dressed as civilians came from Russia and took them." Oleg slapped his forehead with the palm of his hand. "Duh, of course! One of them asked where the third one was, and Skull told them that it wasn't at the church like they had expected. Oh God, did they go after him?"

Alexander scrambled to his feet, ignoring the headache. "Who? Where does he live? Where is his business? What is the model of the car?"

"I only saw him a few times. He has a big factory. Makes different kinds of food—sausages, dumplings, pastries, and things like that. That's why they didn't touch him before. The militias and our Russians would eat at his place. He feeds the poor and homeless near the factory on Saturdays." He glanced at his watch. "It's lunch time already. Did they really go there?" He put his head in his hands.

Alexander snapped his fingers. "Focus, Oleg, don't give up so easily. Where is the factory?"

Oleg pointed out a window. "At the entrance of the city, directly bordering the field. Next to the bus station. I can show you." He started for the door.

"Is there another car we can use?"

Oleg shook his head. "Just a motorcycle."

Alexander held up a hand. "You stay here. You stepped outside to use the bathroom and heard the roar of the motorcycle. I left before you could stop me. That's what you tell them. We must be careful."

Oleg nodded. Alexander walked towards the door. Oleg's hand caught his elbow as he passed. "Wait, one more thing!" he said. "Someone else came this morning. They didn't tell me who he was, just that I should put his things in the closet. I think they might be explosives or something."

"Where is he?"

"He left with them. I got the impression that they all know one another quite well."

Alexander considered the different options available to him and what this most recent development could mean. He got an idea, and returned to his makeshift bed on the floor. He pulled out the pistol and the envelope from under the pillow. He carefully opened the envelope and found a photograph among the instructions and a few Ukrainian passports. He studied the picture, trying to remember if he had seen the face before. Finally, he showed it to Oleg.

"That's him, who is he?" the student asked eagerly.

Alexander shoved the envelope back under the pillow. "No one touches this envelope. If I don't return by midnight, burn it without looking inside. I can't take it with me, and there's no point in hiding it in other places. I'm trusting you, like you trusted me."

Moments later, the roar of the motorcycle was carried away by the wind.

At the entrance to the bus station, Alexander saw a large crowd of women, children, and elderly people slowly walking from the sausage factory to the bus stop. Trying not to attract too much attention, he drove up to a dilapidated house from which he could watch over the factory.

An hour went by with no activity. Two cars and a motorcycle drove up to the factory, but no foreign cars were to be seen. The gate remained open. Finally, a steel-colored BMW drove out of the gate. A man of medium height got out, walked to the gate, and closed it.

Suddenly, a small van with tinted windows pulled up and blocked the road. Alexander hadn't registered it earlier; there had been no signs of activity from it. Six people got out, and Alexander immediately recognized one as the skinhead Demon. *Where is everyone else?* he thought.

Alexander would have liked to wait a few more minutes, but he had no time to lose. Whatever situation was evolving, it was moving too quickly for him to take his time. Brotherhood members surrounded the BMW driver and began to attack him. Someone landed a strong blow to his stomach, it looked like Boa, followed by a fist to the jaw. The driver was bounced around by the Brotherhood, who punched and kicked him without letting him fall to the ground. As the man began to grow limp, Snake and Boa held him up while Demon grabbed him by the neck and yelled in his face.

Alexander raced the motorcycle into the crowd at full speed and braked sharply. The wheels squealed and all eyes were turned to him. Everyone froze at his unexpected intrusion. With a broken mouth and blood on his face and in his eyes, the driver looked at Alexander. He was breathing in sharp gasps. Alexander got off the motorcycle and slowly approached the driver. The Brotherhood members let him go, and eyed Alexander with malice. Boa started to say something to Demon, but the leader shook his head violently and held out his hand as a signal to wait.

"Are you the owner of this sausage factory?" Alexander asked the man, slipping an arm around the man's ribs and lifting him back to his feet.

The broken and bloodied man nodded, glancing nervously towards his attackers.

"What do they want from you?" Alexander nodded toward Demon. The driver just stared at Alexander. "Car? Money?"

The driver slowly nodded. "It's a sin to give bastards like you anything."

"I don't need your car. Neither do these guys." Alexander waved Snake and Boa away. To the driver, he said, "Think you can stand on your own?"

The driver nodded, but Snake and Boa only took a few short steps back, noting how unsteady the man was on his feet.

"I'm new to town, but I've heard about the extent of your generosity and the quality of your products far beyond the border of this town," Alexander said. "That's why I stopped by—to buy some sausage, maybe ten kilograms? So come on, open the gate. I'll make my purchases, and we'll get out of your hair."

The driver stared at Alexander just as coldly as before, unsure what to do.

Demon stepped forward. "I think you arrived at the wrong time and at the wrong place. We take orders from Moscow, the Kremlin. You may have been sent here, but you aren't the one making decisions."

Before Demon could raise his weapon, Alexander spun and wrenched the machine gun from his hands and drove the butt squarely against Demon's cheek. Demons, eyes rolled as his body twisted around and collapsed limply to the pavement.

Alexander's booted foot pivoted quickly, hitting Boa's locked knees from behind and sending him reaching for the ground as he fell. As Boa scrambled back up, Snake yelled in pain, trying to pull a knife out of his own leg. He grabbed for his gun, but a punch to the back of his neck sent Snake to all fours on the asphalt, moaning as blood dripped from his open mouth. Slowly he sunk down.

"Behind you!" the driver shouted.

Before Alexander could turn around, he felt something wet and warm splatter his hands and cheek. At the same time, he was vaguely aware of the *crack* of a rifle. Instinctively, he jumped to the side, and rolled. He wasn't sure where the shot had come from, and he pressed his back against the BMW, scanning the surrounding buildings for signs. A body slid down the hood of the BMW. A corpse with a skull demolished by the explosive bullet fell to the ground beside him, a Spetsnaz knife still clutched in the right hand. Alexander toed it out of the way.

The air fell silent. Alexander decided to take his chance, and hoped that whoever had fired the shot was entirely on his side. "Help me drag them to the van," he said, gesturing to the bodies. The owner stood there for a moment, a glazed look in his eyes. Alexander yelled his instructions again, and the man stumbled in shock to Demon, grunting as he slung his unconscious body over his shoulder and carried him to the Brotherhood's van.

"Do you have a first aid kit in your car?" Alexander asked.

"Yes, but it won't be enough for all of them. Our housemaid used to be the head physician at the hospital. I don't live far from here. She'll bandage them up."

"A doctor would be good, but not at the house. Bring her here; let her take care of them in the back of the van. And this one," Alexander nodded toward the dead man, "he needs to be taken to the morgue."

CHAPTER 8

Colonel Karpenko's field office was located on the first floor of a partially bombed-out garment factory—his men had pushed aside the boxes of textiles and tools to make room for military equipment. It wasn't an ideal situation, but the place served as a functional operational center. Arms and ammunition were piled next to the Colonel's desk, where he sat flipping through paperwork, and the cracked windows all around were plastered with film.

The office door burst open and a Sergeant rushed in, short of breath.

"Sorry, Comrade Colonel, but two Moskals are demanding that I connect them with the commander—with you. Something about Mikola, a Ukrainian?" The Sergeant was pushed aside as the two men entered the office, eager to just get to business.

"Mikola! We finally found you," one of the men joyfully shouted before hugging the Colonel.

The young Sergeant stared perplexedly at the Moskals.

"Sergeant, bring us some coffee," the Colonel said, "and something to go with it."

Peter, Victor, and Mikola sat around the table.

"I didn't think I'd ever see you again after Crimea," Mikola said.

Victor nodded. "That was a turning point, my friend. At first, we thought that everything would end there, but how wrong we were. Eastern Ukraine exploded, and we had to get out of there. We had seen enough in Chechnya. So Peter and I decided to fire ourselves and come visit you. Who knows, maybe we'll be able to help with something. Nobody in the Ministry of Defense even noticed our report of dismissal."

Peter chimed in, "We owe you so much, Mikola. When we found out you were here, we had to come."

Mikola smiled at Peter's words, then turned to Victor and asked, "Fight against your own? Against Russians?"

"No, not our own," Peter said. "We are Siberians, they are Moskal bastards. We will fight against the occupiers, those taking the land of our brotherly people. We don't have anything in common with those Kremlin bastards running over Ukraine. The Kremlin is not Russia, nor is it Siberia. We won't be their puppets."

Victor nodded in agreement. "Just sign us up for your regiment and we'll fight together. But we have one request."

"Let's hear it," Mikola asked, nodding his head. His eyes squinted to look these men up and down with mild amusement, impressed and yet also wearied by the two firebrands.

"When we liberate Ukraine from all of Putin's thugs," Victor answered, "you must come to Siberia with your battalion to help us liberate our territory from this Kremlin mafia. We too are tired of paying tribute to the Moscow horde. Our people—in some places people are living as if it's still the nineteenth century. All they have is vodka, the damned TV with Putin's face on every channel, and no future."

Mikola smiled. "Well, I can't speak for an entire battalion, but I will definitely come—if I'm still alive." He paused, thinking back to the day that fate had led the three of them to the same path. Peter and Victor had been solid men, and he trusted them. "We have several platoons of Siberians and Kuban's here. Where do you want to be?"

Peter and Victor both said, "With the Siberians."

Mikola nodded, not surprised. "I had a feeling you would choose that way. As for weaponry—"

"We have our own," Peter interrupted. "Two machine guns and a sniper rifle. It'll be enough for now. They're over there in a bag by the door to your office."

"How did you even get in here without Ukrainian passports? Not to mention your weapons."

"Simple," Victor shrugged. "We paid a Ukrainian brother with some green ones and he drove us right to your door. By the way, here's the number of his car. Who knows whom else he drives around there. Tell your guys to pull him up."

Mikola wasn't one to waste time. He prided himself on his ability to make snap decisions, and decided that there was no sense in waiting any longer. He stood up, ordered his new soldiers to pick up their weapons, and took them to the platoon barracks. He introduced them to Russians, Georgians, Belarusians, and even Chechens. The soldiers were a bit confused by the sudden arrival of two apparent Moskals who seemed to know their Colonel so well, but they had other things on their mind and quickly went about their duties.

The Colonel pulled out a map from his breast pocket, unfolded it, and spread it out on a nearby table. "Let's put you to work, my friends. Over the past few days, I have received word that some kind of saboteur group is operating in this neighborhood." He gestured to an area slightly to the west of their encampment. "They shoot at civilians, even at children. They're creating a red terror and are working together with the Russian media. Every terrorist attack that they create, their Russian news investigators report it as if it was perpetrated by the Ukrainians."

Peter looked at Victor. "Care to take a little walk around our new neighborhood?"

Victor grinned. "I think so. Get to know the area better, exchange a few words with the local population…" He nodded. "We'll try to do something. We won't let you down."

Satisfied, Mikola put the map back in his pocket and returned to his makeshift office, having given word that they should report to the Commander for a ride into Donetsk.

The Commander of the group drove them to the outskirts of the city, stopping about three kilometers from the suburbs so as not to attract attention. This far out, it was ghostly quiet, but Peter and Victor could sense the tension in the area ahead.

"When should I pick you up?" the Commander asked.

"Don't worry about it," Peter said with an edge of greedy anticipation.

"We'll get ourselves back," Victor added.

They made their way toward the city—or what was left of it. The vegetation was all but burnt up, and broken roofs peeked out over the hills. The ground was littered with shards of broken glass, scraps of paper, and garbage. As they turned down a large street, they saw a commercial building three hundred meters from them and headed toward it. When they were close enough, they saw that a group of people had gathered in front of the building. Peter stopped and gestured for Victor to follow him.

Peter skirted around a dilapidated van to some stairs on the outside of a small storehouse, which appeared to be empty, across from the crowd.

"What's going on?" Victor whispered as they clambered up the stairs.

"Something doesn't feel right up ahead. Did you see those people? They were all staring at something...I want to find out what, and I want a good view." He pointed his finger upwards.

Within a few seconds, they had found their way to the roof. They dropped down, crawled to the edge and slowly peeked over the lip.

Peter whistled softly. "Something is definitely going down; that poor guy is getting quite the beating." There was a screech and smoke of tires, and a motorcycle pulled into view. A man hopped down, and approached the disturbance with quick and authoritative steps.

Victor pulled out his sniper rifle and pointed the scope toward the crowd.

"I don't believe it," Victor whispered. "Remember Sevastopol—that young Lieutenant Colonel?"

Peter nodded. "Yeah, the one who had us throw the lady journalist on the bus. Weirdest order we've ever gotten, for sure. And?"

Suddenly, the young Lieutenant Colonel sprang into action below, spinning wildly and landing hard blows on the men in military garb who had just been beating the man on the ground. Victor handed the sniper rifle to Peter, who peered through the scope. In the blink of an eye, Peter unexpectedly pulled on the bolt and fired off a shot.

"Idiot!" Victor shouted. "What'd you do? Why'd you—"

Peter shoved the rifle back into Victor's hands. "Look for yourself."

Victor pressed his eye to the scope. A man in a camouflage uniform with a Spetsnaz knife in his right hand stumbled and wavered for a brief second, then fell to his knees and collapsed on the ground next to Alexander's feet. His head had been split open by Peter's well-placed shot. The Lieutenant Colonel was crouched next to a BMW, wiping blood off his hands and face and looking around furtively.

Victor sighed with relief. "I thought that you got the Lieutenant Colonel. Sorry."

Peter punched him in the arm. "To hell with your apology. You didn't see how he stormed at those six. Who the heck is he anyway? KGB, GRU, SBU, or maybe CIA? I don't know, but he should live. It seems that he's a normal guy."

"Yeah, a normal guy who can take on mercenaries with his bare hands. Anyways, nice shot."

"He didn't tell on us that time in Sevastopol when we told him everything. Something tells me is that he may be one of us. Damn, I've never been so sentimental." Peter wiped an imaginary tear from his cheek.

Victor chuckled and looked back. "And after all that, he's bandaging them up."

"I'm telling you," Peter said, "there's something about this guy."

CHAPTER 9

The morning after the run-in at the factory, Alexander left the house to walk through the garden. It was a rare and beautiful garden, left untouched in an otherwise war-torn city. From here, he could watch neatly dressed men, women, and children walking through the streets with purpose, all heading somewhere. He briefly wondered if Stepan, the sausage factory businessman, was walking somewhere with purpose that morning too.

Footsteps sounded behind him, and Alexander saw Oleg's reflection in the window of a nearby house. Without turning to greet the young man, he said, "All quiet inside?"

"He won't forgive you for what you did to them."

"No, I don't suppose so." Alexander rocked on his heels.

"Demon is ready to shoot any Ukrainian he can find. I don't think that he will leave you or the businessman alive either."

Alexander simply nodded. "Where are they headed to with such determination?" He indicated the people walking along the street.

Oleg stretched his hand towards the still-standing church. "They have a morning service every Sunday. Ever been in a church?" When Alexander shook his head no, Oleg said, "I've been there twice. There is something attractive about it."

"I'm sure it would be a sight to see," Alexander said, almost wistfully. "But not today." He turned to face Oleg, suddenly very stiff and professional. "I have to look over all of the 'toys' that Graf brought. You go remind the lads that training is at twelve midnight, sharp. We've got some new modified explosives, some from the Americans and their allies. I don't want one idiot to blow us all up.

"Bring all those explosions to the printing house which is on the side of the town. I will explain training and mission details over there, not here. Be very, very careful and don't forget to lock up the door. Make sure you hear the key."

Thirty minutes later, Oleg was hurrying to find Alexander.

"I told them," he said quickly, "just like you asked. But Demon—well, he reacted about as well as you might expect. Said he didn't need explosives to take care of business."

"Where is he now?" Alexander balled his fists in frustration. He rushed through the rooms of the house towards the front door.

Oleg hurried to follow. "Last I saw, he was headed toward the church. With his machine gun."

"The businessman—the one from the other day. Does he go to that church?"

Oleg shrugged. "I don't know if he attends services, but he sometimes brings food to feed people in need."

Alexander was already grabbing his gun and heading out the door. Over his shoulder he shouted, "Oleg, organize all those 'toys'—just like I told you."

The day was sunny—not even a cloud of smoke from exploding shells was visible in the sky. It was a rare silence for the joyful parishioners. As Alexander raced toward the church, he scanned the parking lot. The businessman's car was not there. It wasn't around back either. For a moment, he was relieved. Then he remembered the type of character Demon was; obsessive, cruel, and prideful.

Where was Demon? Had he driven to the businessman's house? A sense of dread washed over him. That idiot would shoot the man's entire family.

He went back to the front of the church. A crowd of parishioners was leaving. For a moment, his gaze lingered on a pretty young woman dressed in traditional Ukrainian clothing. She had a blue and yellow shawl around her neck. She was pregnant and talking animatedly to a young girl who was barely school age. The little girl was a striking copy of her mother.

A joyful Tatyana flashed before Alexander's eyes, and flames of family warmth erupted in his heart. A fleeting smile passed over his lips. "Later, man," he told himself through gritted teeth. "For now, there's war." He scanned the crowd.

Still no Demon. No Brotherhood at all. He decided that he should check Stepan's house, but he did not have a car and he knew that it was too great a distance to travel on foot. Alexander hurried past the church and into the far road, but not one car was on the road. Just his luck.

Suddenly, a short burst of gunfire rang out from the church, followed by screams. Alexander spun around, his heart sinking as he saw the same cheerful brunette falling to her knees with one hand weakly clutching her belly as the other reached desperately for the ground. Bloody spots already covered the snow-white embroidery on her chest. The blue and yellow silk shawl slipped from her shoulders and tripped lightly in the breeze before being carried upwards, along with the young mother's last breath, to the bottomless blue heaven. Alexander watched as the breeze quieted and the scarf dropped limply across the woman's face.

Alexander's eyes scanned the periphery as he flattened himself against the side of the church. People were running in all directions, and it was hard to make out details in the chaos. He tried to make himself unobtrusive; he had no doubt that, given the chance, Demon would shoot him. Demon was nowhere to be seen, but he had begun catching flashes of men in uniform.

He finally stepped up to the dead woman. Dark curls spread out on the gravel. Her snow-white skin, black eyebrows and lashes emphasized the uniqueness of her beauty. The sun's rays were reflecting in her open, frozen blue eyes. Crimson blood stained the blue and yellow scarf. Alexander felt the infinite depth of those colors as he scanned the area: the beautiful blueness of the Ukrainian sky, the abundant yellow wheat fields, and the deep price of freedom that the entire nation must bear.

Alexander glanced at the woman one more time, this time noticing the blood on her stomach. He thought he saw a ripple of movement, followed by another, although much weaker. Alexander looked away, afraid that he might be sick at the senseless loss of life.

He turned to find the barrel of the machine gun pointed in his face. Demon's crazy eyes were at the other end.

"Now what, Uninvited Commander? Are you ready to accompany this Ukrainian bitch?" He kicked his toe toward the lifeless body. "Too bad she wasn't wearing colors like mine." He popped his collar with his left hand. A wide St. George ribbon displaying the colors of a Colorado beetle was wrapped around his neck. "We'll shed a lot of their blood today. We'll celebrate with a funeral feast! The guys are on their way."

"Neither you nor your Kremlin vampires will drink any more of their blood," Alexander said in a low voice. "The wild dogs will have a funeral feast for you." Alexander closed his eyes for a moment, the image of those blue lifeless eyes burned in the darkness. He saw Tatyana's face. It could have been her.

As he opened his eyes again, the memory of Tatyana reading on their way from Valentin's house came back to him –the fighter of the Ukrainian liberation army mutilated in a faraway prison and her executioner—the drunk officer of the Soviet army.

Alexander took a breath and a sense of calm purpose overcame him. He no longer had to look at Demon. He was fully in tune with every movement, every breath of the man. He felt how Demon was moving his left hand toward the machine gun and how his right index finger began to slightly squeeze the trigger. Alexander moved swiftly towards Demon, every fiber in his body flowing free with explosive power.

In a swift circular motion, Alexander simultaneously redirected the barrel of the machine gun with his right hand while sending a paralyzing cross with his left. A short round of gunfire burst forth. The shot rushed by his right ear in a deafening blast. His ears rang. Alexander pressed forward, sending his right fist deep into Demon's solar plexus. He had a brief image of Demon's face, his teeth gritted in pain and surprise. The man stiffened violently, his body reacting to the punch, and Alexander delivered a crushing kick to his throat. There was a dull crunch as Alexander's heavy boot connected. Demon fell spread eagle onto his back. A wet gurgling sound came from his bloodied mouth, eyes rolling and yet fingers still grasping instinctively at the gun. Alexander stepped on his wrist to relieve the weapon.

Churchgoers huddled in the awning stood transfixed, staring at the two men. A few crossed themselves.

Alexander tore the ribbon from Demon's neck, wiped his hands on it, and threw it back on the dead man's face. He noticed a broken chain and a metal badge on Demon's chest. He bent down and snatched it up. The badge had Demon's real name and the code number of his squad: D.B.N - Diversionary Battalion of New Russia.

Boa came charging around the corner of the church, gun outstretched. "You goddamned bastard. This you did in vain," he croaked and spat loudly on the ground. "Trading the life of our brother for that Ukrainian."

At the same moment: "Put away the gun," a stern voice rang out.

Alexander turned to see a tall and weathered-looking priest moving closer to Boa, his hands held out in a reassuring motion. The man wore a black cassock, and a gilded cross of impressive size hung from a long chain around his neck, indicating the Ukrainian Orthodox faith. From around the same corner that Boa had emerged, more members of the Brotherhood were approaching.

"Go to hell, priest," Boa snarled.

"I've been there—in Afghanistan," the priest replied calmly, still moving slowly forward. He had sandy hair and narrow cheeks that betrayed his athleticism while hinting at a hard-fought life. Alexander had spent most of his adult life around military men, and he knew one when he saw one.

Boa drew the gun away from Alexander and swung it to send a round into the priest, but it was too late. The priest moved with unexpected fluidity and speed. Lunging forward, the priest's black robe shifted and the gun jolted up and towards the gravel several feet away, followed by a stunned Boa after the priest's elbow knocked the prayer from Boa's lips. The Brotherhood rushed up to catch an unconscious Boa just before he hit the ground. Alexander caught the gun and pointed it at the Brotherhood.

"Lower your weapons," Alexander commanded. "Unless you want to join Demon," he said, jerking his head in the direction of the two bodies—the woman clothed in white, and the skinhead. The Brotherhood remained silent. "Good."

"Now," he continued, "all of you meet me in the printing house at 24:00 sharp. Anyone who doesn't show up will be shot on sight."

The Brotherhood stared down his barrel in contemptuous silence.

"Do I have to ask each one of you personally?" he snarled.

Several voices chimed in. "Understood, sir." Their leader gone, the group of criminals were without courage, and quickly caved to Alexander's authority.

"Then disperse!"

As the Brotherhood departed, Alexander stretched a hand out to the priest and introduced himself.

"Michael," the priest said, introducing himself. "Please, step inside with me. A tragedy has occurred, and a decision must be made."

"Did she have a husband?" Alexander asked as they passed the young woman's body. Several parishioners were gathered around it. Women with tears in their eyes wiped blood from the woman's tender face with lace handkerchiefs. Several men approached with a stretcher that they had fashioned to bear the body to the church, and a grandmotherly figure held the little girl's head as she clutched the front of her dress and looked on in silence.

Michael nodded. "He's in Rostov for the weekend. Visiting his sick mother."

"He's Russian?"

Again Michael nodded. "Grew up without a father. Now his daughter has to grow up without a mother."

The two men watched blankly as the parishioners gathered up the body.

"So if it isn't a secret, where did you learn to take down a man so easily?" Alexander asked the priest.

Michael shook his head. "I wish that I had left that skill in Afghanistan—I served as a colonel."

"You didn't want to become a general?"

Michael fingered the cross around his neck. "There is no higher rank for me than that of a priest, and the sacred acts of serving God and my people. It just gets very difficult when two people live in the same flesh: a former officer of the foreign intelligence of the USSR, and a priest of a free and independent Ukraine."

"Who are your people?"

"The Ukrainians. I was born and raised in the Rivne region, but the doors to my heart are open to everyone—even those who are killing us." His voice was heavy with the pain of years, years that had seen far too many perish that should have lived.

"Listen, we're leaving tonight, and I will do everything possible for it to be a permanent departure, but I do have a small request." Alexander stepped closer to Michael and lowered his voice. "Amidst all of these gangsters is a student from St. Petersburg. Oleg. He came here with good intentions, but he fell for the propaganda. Please help him return to St. Petersburg, to his mother and sisters there."

Michael was already shaking his head. "It doesn't matter what I do. At the border, the Russians will shoot him, even if he is one of their own. They don't allow living Russian soldiers to come back to Russia. Only as 'cargo 200.'"

Alexander gripped the man's shoulder. "Please. I can't be there. There must be something you can do."

Finally the priest nodded. "I will try."

"That's all I can ask. Thank you." Alexander shook his hand. "I will send him to you tonight. Keep him with you. And let's pretend that this conversation never happened." He started to leave, then stopped and turned back to the priest. "Do you know where I can buy a cheap car from someone?"

"Take my car. It's not new, of course, but it still drives."

"I must buy it. I will not be able to return it."

The priest pointed to a small building. "In my office, you'll find car keys on the table. It's the Moskvich behind the church. God sent me this one. He'll send me another. You'll be in my prayers."

Michael turned and crossed the threshold into the sacred house. Alexander watched him go in sadness. Despite everything he had been though, he still cared for his flock. It would be a night of mourning for the girl, but Alexander couldn't help but think that the poor souls here were in good hands.

Alexander did as instructed and gathered the keys. The Moskvich was old and dingy, but seemed reliable. It started up with no problems, and thirty minutes later, Alexander stopped by the factory owner's home and told him about the young Ukrainian woman's death.

"I know I have no right to ask—"

"You saved my life," Stepan interjected. "I am indebted to you. What do you need?" There was underlying anger in his voice, mingled with a sense of resolve.

"Not for me, but the young woman's family. Can you help bury her with honor? And perhaps get her husband a job—at least for the sake of the young daughter?"

"Done."

Alexander shook his hand. "We won't see each other again."

Stepan walked Alexander away from the house.

"Can I ask you why?"

"I am leaving for Kiev tonight," Alexander said.

When Stepan saw the Moskvich, he laughed.

"In this car? You won't make it a hundred kilometers before the wheels are flying off." He held out his keys. "Take my car."

"Stepan, I don't have money to pay for this car, and also I'm not sure if I will be able to return it to you."

"Don't worry; terrorists are going to take it sooner or later anyways. If I don't have something new and shiny for them to steal, the better for me."

Alexander knew he was right. But he had things he had to take care of before his departure, and didn't want to attract attention.

"Tell you what; leave the keys under the seat tonight. But don't be surprised to find a Moskvich in its place in the morning." He thanked the man and headed to the printing house on the outskirts of town.

It was an old, rundown, one-story brick building. Despite the war and decrepitude, the doors and windows were still in place. He opened the padlock, walked in, and closed the door behind him.

The explosive devices were in the correct positions, as he had instructed Oleg. Alexander lingered in the printing house for the rest of the day.

Thirty seconds before the midnight deadline, the Brotherhood shuffled in. Alexander explained their mission.

"Our first target is a Ukrainian hospital on the western edge of town," he said. He hardened his voice. "Demon is no longer with us, for a simple reason. He acted without my approval and did not attack an appropriate military target. We will be able to send a message when the mines detonate and destroy the infrastructure."

The members of the Brotherhood who had witnessed Demon's death shuffled their feet awkwardly. *Good*, Alexander thought. *It looks like they finally fear me.*

After brief instructions, Alexander asked each of the men to describe their various skill sets. Some claimed to have excellent aim, while others lauded their hand-to-hand combat skills. When he got to Student, though, he asked, "Have you ever cut the throat of a living person?"

Student turned pale and shook his head. The Brotherhood laughed.

Vampire called out to Student and raised his vest, pointing at a large tattoo on his chest. "Know what this is?"

"A St. George ribbon and a bat," Student answered timidly, glancing sidelong at Alexander.

"You're the bat. This is a vampire who loves to drink fresh blood!" Vampire laughed. Clearly he'd gotten his nickname from his tattoo. "But don't worry, you're one of us."

"I don't know how I even got here. I never had any special training."

Alexander held up a hand. "The best training is practice. So today you will get good practice, under my direction. First, you will cut the priest's throat. When you finish your work in the church, you'll join Boa's group to blow up the hospital." Alexander looked at Boa. "Your team will cover it with mines, but Student will personally push the button. Understood?"

"But the injured, the children," Student said quietly.

"They're not our people. The hospital is important material for propaganda, and we must use it effectively. The enemy is the enemy, regardless of their physical condition, age, or gender."

Alexander stared at Student, reading the disappointment in the young man's eyes. He felt terrible about putting Student through this, but he couldn't give up the charade yet. "The assignment must be fulfilled. There are going to be a lot of fireworks tonight and well into tomorrow, in theaters and on buses. We also have to make the most of our Russian media contacts. Student, you're responsible for this as well. Invite them to all the events and give them the professional and legal language to use during an interview about the animal, fascist Banderas. Understood?"

Student nodded glumly.

"And give the interview in English for our international television stations." Alexander raised an eyebrow. "See? You weren't sent to us by mistake. We need your unique skillset, college boy."

"Let me watch over Student in the church," Boa said through clenched teeth. "I will tear that priest into pieces."

"You had that opportunity just a couple of hours ago. You should be thankful that he didn't break your skull. I don't want a second failed attempt. Student will fulfill your desires—with my help, of course." Alexander signaled for Student to grab his gear and headed to the exit. "You men will review your assignments and understand how to position and time these explosives," he called over his shoulder. "No more screw ups on my watch."

Student sullenly followed Alexander to the car and they drove to the church in silence. About 200 meters from the church, Alexander pulled the car onto the shoulder and turned it off. He turned to Oleg.

"Will you be able to do what we talked about?"

"This is not what I came here for," Oleg said, his voice cracking. "I did not sign up for this. I am not a terrorist. If that means I can't return home, then just shoot me now. It'll be easier for us both. I wouldn't be able to live with myself."

"Give me your gun, pistol, and knife."

Oleg shoved his weapons into Alexander's hands, his eyes watering with anger. Alexander got out of the car, put the weapons in the trunk, and returned to the driver's seat.

"Forgive me for the charade. I just needed to make sure you were the man I thought you were."

Oleg shook his head in confusion. "What are you talking about?"

Alexander tried to reassure him. "You've made the right decision. You won't need the weapons. The priest is waiting for you. You will be under his command. Help him with everything he needs."

Alexander looked out the front window, remembering the tragedy from earlier that day. The scene would haunt him for the rest of his days, he was sure of it. Again he thought of Tatyana.

"Demon really messed things up today." He tried to block the images from his mind, but they were too intense. He looked around to Oleg.

"The priest is good and trustworthy. You can believe him. Maybe he will help you to reconnect with your family. Continue your education in some other country. People need uncompromising lawyers and judges like you." Alexander placed a hand on Oleg's shoulder. "You stood with honor before the bullet. Try to stand strong in front of the dollar as well. Trust me, this is much harder."

"I won't let you down," Oleg whispered. He got out of the car and headed for the church, his step practically gleeful as he walked toward a new beginning. Alexander watched him go with a smile.

It was long after nightfall when Alexander returned to the factory owner's house. The gates were open. As Alexander walked tentatively through, Stepan appeared onto the patio and invited him inside. Alexander politely refused.

"I know you said we wouldn't see each other again. Sorry about popping up like this. I drew a map with the backroads, I figured you would need it. Don't worry, it's trustworthy," Stepan said. "Everything you need is in the glove compartment. Food is in the trunk."

Alexander thanked him and transferred his gear into the BMW. He opened up the glove compartment. "What is this?" He removed a thick stack of Ukrainian money.

"For fuel and travel expenses."

"My dear friend, thank you." Alexander got into the car, and then rolled down the window. "Don't leave your house tonight. Also, stay away from the Russian media tomorrow." He backed down the drive before the man could ask any questions, flashed the headlights in goodbye, and disappeared into the hellish darkness of the unlit streets.

Alexander parked the car in the driveway of a destroyed cottage not too far from the printing house. There was only silence all around and not a single soul. Exactly what he was hoping for.

He pulled the map with the backroads out of his pocket and studied it carefully, memorizing every route around the DNR and the Ukrainian roadblocks. Then he flicked open a lighter and turned the map into ashes.

He spent a few more minutes in his car, running through his head what he was about to do. It was necessary, but not easy. Then he shook himself from his doubts, eyes refocusing on rubble-strewn street, and opened the car door.

"Okay guys," Alexander said walking into the printing house, "just reminding you, we have five main objectives." The Brotherhood members took their places around the table. "The hospital, the museum, theater, and two public transportation buses; make sure they have passengers during commute times." He placed two small bags on the table. "In these are different fragments of Ukrainian and Bandera imagery. Leave them around your objective points, in trash cans or other places as if you discarded them during an escape. Also, splinters from the American mines will be good proof of their involvement as well as NATO's. Our media will know to look for them. Everything must be clean. If you are caught placing these materials, leave no witnesses."

"Will there be enough explosives?" Boa asked.

Alexander nodded. "Graf made sure of that." His phone rang, startling them all. Alexander felt an icy chill and looked at the number. This call was not a part of his plan. "Stay in your spots until I return. Do not leave the building."

He stepped outside, closed the door behind him, and hastily walked towards his car. The telephone conversation was short. It was general Trofimov from Sevastopol. He was ordered to not return to Crimea, but to travel directly to Moscow. Alexander hung up, and looked around a few more times. Seeing nobody, he got in the car and coasted out of the driveway with his headlights off. He turned around the corner of a large, partially destroyed three-story house and stopped, letting the engine idle.

He tilted his head back against the seat, looked up to the roof, and quietly whispered, "If you exist, forgive me for this sin. But it would be an even greater sin to leave these blood suckers alive."

He slid the remote from his pocket and pressed the button quickly, before he could change his mind. The explosion shook the car. Flames bust through the windows and doors of the printing house, scattering debris and charred, unrecognizable pieces of flesh in all directions.

Without looking back, Alexander pressed on the gas. He only turned on his headlights when he pulled onto the highway. No matter how fast he was going, the flames from the burning printing house remained in the BMW's mirrors.

CHAPTER 10

Before entering Ukrainian-controlled territory, Alexander stopped to bury his weapons and change into his civilian clothing. He buried his uniform as well. After rechecking his documents, he kept the Ukrainian citizen passport that he needed and hid the rest of the documents in a gap beneath the steering wheel.

That night had flown by quickly. He had driven like a madman, trying not to think about the bloodshed he had left behind. By the time he reached Kiev safely, it was around 2:00 PM. He stopped near an old payphone on Khreshchatyk and called Tatyana at her office.

When he heard her soft, warm voice on the other end, Alexander smiled. Relief washed over him. Somehow, he had been afraid that she wouldn't answer, that she had somehow been injured or killed with the poor woman in Donetsk. Who could have thought that everything would change because of one Kremlin thug? Now he felt like a foreigner in his beloved city. He had even needed to use a stranger's passport to remain undercover when, not too long ago, he had been one of their own.

Alexander deepened his voice and added an aristocratic accent when he spoke.

"May I talk to Tatyana?"

"Yes, speaking," Tatyana answered professionally.

"I need to pass on some materials to your printing press—to you personally, in fact."

"Of course," Tatyana said no hint of recognition in her voice. "We're on the second floor."

"Actually, it would be better if you come downstairs to meet me."

"Alright, but you will have to wait a few moments." Ever the negotiator.

"No worries, I can wait."

Ten minutes later, Tatyana appeared. She was wearing a crisp pencil skirt and blouse. Seeing her again brought a wave of peace and a gentle smile to Alexander's face. She lit up when she saw him leaning against the BMW. Her heels tapped quickly on the pavement as she skipped to hug him tightly and spread joyful kisses all over his face. "Why didn't you tell me it was you? Come inside so I can introduce you to my colleagues…and nice car!" She took him by the hand and started to lead him to the door.

"Wait." He pulled her to a stop. "Here in Kiev, I have a different last name. Karpenko." He offered her a lopsided smile. "I finally became a Ukrainian. I just speak in Russian."

"It's okay! You will speak in Ukrainian soon. But how did you become a Ukrainian?"

Alexander changed his tone into a more serious one. "First, I need some help. You once told me that you know an American who works in the embassy, and that sometimes he asks you for more detailed explanations of some of your articles about operations in the ATO zone." The ATO zone was shorthand for the terrorist-ridden area surrounding Donetsk.

"Would you be able to set up a meeting with him and give him a note to pass on to someone else in the embassy?"

"I could get us both an invitation to the embassy if you'd prefer." She squeezed his hand, but her eyes betrayed a growing sense of cautious curiosity.

"Darling, I'm a Russian officer in enemy territory." He glanced around as he spoke, as if to prove his point. "Everything is under surveillance there—American, Ukrainian, and not to mention Russian cameras. I can't be seen there." He looked back into her eyes. "It would probably be better for you to stay away as well."

She shrugged in agreement. "If you say so. What do you want me to do then?"

"Call him and tell him that you have some interesting material for him. Have him come to the editing house. Don't call him from your cell phone. Use the office phone." He handed her the envelope. "Don't lose it, and make sure it doesn't get into anyone else's hands—destroy it if it comes to that. I'll be waiting for you in the car, over there, by Café Lakomka on the corner."

Tatyana held up a hand to shield her eyes from the sun as she looked down the street towards the café. "I remember it. Where did you get this?"

"There is no time for that now. After the meeting, wait about fifteen minutes after he leaves, then head over to Lakomka and buy yourself a coffee. After that, sit at my table, we'll talk for a few minutes, and then you can ask for a ride."

She laughed. "What, are we spies now?"

Alexander shifted on his feet uncomfortably. "He may have a tail. Russian GRU or FSB. He's from the embassy after all. Best to be safe, right? Just do everything as I have told you. Assume that all of your conversations, especially with the American embassy, are listened to and recorded by Russian Special Forces." He gave her a quick kiss on the cheek. "I've got to go. Any chance we can get this done today would be nice. Oh, and whisper in his ear that this note is from your fiancé. I think that will significantly speed up the process."

They embraced once more, in the shadow of the office building. Tatyana looked up and down the street exaggeratedly, clearly taking to her new role as spy. He shook his head, smiling, and turned away—but not before giving her a pointed reminder of the seriousness of the situation. He drove around for an hour or so to account for the time it would take Tatyana to schedule the appointment. Then he took a position at café Lakomka, next to the outdoor tables.

Forty-five minutes later, a Ford with diplomatic license plates pulled up in front of the editing house. An older man wearing a somewhat wrinkled suit stepped out and went inside. After twenty minutes, he returned to his car and left.

Tatyana exited the editing house seventeen minutes later and Alexander watched over the edge of his newspaper as she strolled passed him without a hint of recognition. She had put on large sunglasses and had an intelligent air about her. A few moments later, she came out carrying a coffee. She glanced at the other customers before asking Alexander if she could take the chair next to him. Sipping her coffee, she casually inquired as to what he was reading and struck up some small talk about the road repairs and how she took her car to the shop that morning after driving over some debris the workers had left on the streets. "They should really pay more attention!" she declared with a little too much enthusiasm.

Alexander got the hint, "Do you plan to take the bus home?"

"Yes," said Tatyana. "Unless *by chance* you are heading in the same direction?"

Alexander smiled at her clever charade. They both stood up and Alexander led the way to his car, opening the passenger door for her as she sat gracefully, turned, and slid her legs inside.

When they had gone a reasonable distance, Tatyana held out a piece of paper. "He wrote down this address and drew how to get there. It's not far from here, on the coast of the Dnepr. He'll be waiting there for you in two hours."

"That gives us time to grab a bite."

Tatyana frowned. "He said that he would be waiting for you, not us."

"That is his oversight, I am inviting you. You are an excellent spy."

This made her very happy, and they shared a pleasant dinner at a quiet and nondescript restaurant. He evaded Tatyana's questions about where he had been, and she knew enough to stop asking after a while. After finishing lunch, they drove to a nine-story building on the shore of the Dnepr. Alexander checked the address once again, looking up through the windshield of the BMW. The apartment number he'd given was on the second floor. They got out, and made their way up. Alexander pushed the doorbell after scanning the corridor to make sure that they weren't being watched—at least, that no one was hiding around the corner. An elderly woman with a cane slowly opened the door.

"I'm sorry. I must have the wrong address," Alexander said, confused.

"Not at all, Alexander," the woman said with a smile. "They're waiting for you." She pointed down the hall. "In the living room."

Alexander and Tatyana looked over the woman's shoulder in the direction that she had indicated. The wrinkled-suit man poked his head into the hallway. He stepped out, smiling, and stretched a hand to Tatyana. "Well this is unexpected, dear Tatyana."

He shook Alexander's hand as well. "I asked her to keep me company," he told the American.

"Of course. My name is Robert, and it is a pleasure to see you both."

Introductions out of the way, he ushered them further down the hall, toward the living room. The walls of this already narrow passageway were covered in nondescript paintings on one side and bookshelves on the other. The books were all in Russian, Alexander noticed.

"So you passed my note to Bill Brown?" Alexander asked quickly, stepping closer to make sure he was heard.

Without turning around, Robert replied, "Absolutely. I read it right away."

Alexander cocked his head and stopped walking. "You mean Bill Brown read it," he clarified.

Robert chuckled and turned to the confused officer. "My boy, I *am* Bill Brown."

Alexander immediately felt a spark of distrust.

"Please, step into the living room," Robert said reassuringly. "Let's get everything out into the open."

Alexander entered the room, but quickly drew up short, dumbfounded. The Colonel from Belbek Airfield sat at a small table. Before Alexander could say anything, Tatyana pushed into the room.

"I know you! From Sevastopol, at Belbek—you let them take me away and put me on the bus to Yalta!"

The Colonel stood. "My name's James. Nice to meet you officially."

"I don't understand," Robert said, looking from James to Tatyana.

Tatyana sniffed in indignation. "And those thugs threatened to shoot everyone if they let me off the bus before Yalta."

Alexander and James could no longer hold back their laughter.

"Darling," Alexander said, pulling Tatyana aside slightly. "Promise you won't get mad, but I was the masked one who gave them the order to send you to Yalta." When she tried to step away from him, he held her elbow firmly. "I didn't have any other choice in that circumstance. I couldn't risk you being there. It was better that my guys carry you off than for the Russian Cossacks to drag you by your hair down the streets."

Tatyana was convinced enough to sit down, but stiffly. Alexander followed, and soon they were all seated tentatively around the old card table which occupied the middle of the room. Alexander scanned the Russian books that adorned the shelves in there as well. There were thick shutters over the single window. It was utilitarian, but not sparse. *Perfect for an agent*, Alexander thought.

"You can't blame the man," James resumed. "I would have done the exact same thing in his place."

Tatyana paused, then asked "So tell me—who are you exactly?"

"I am on your side, born in America but Ukrainian by blood. I come from a military background and was stationed here after the 2008 summit at Bucharest. Our government grew concerned after the statements made by President Yushchenko, we correctly suspected at that time that Putin would not allow Ukraine to join NATO as some of your leaders had hoped."

"You Americans have such foresight" Alexander interjected, leaning back in his chair with arms crossed in front of his chest.

"Were we wrong?" James replied, looking straight at Alexander.

"The assassination attempt in 2004 by dioxin had not worked on Yuschenko, however, two years later, after Bucharest summit, Putin found the way to install Yanukovych. Putin is playing the long game. You do realize who is controlling Ukrainian policy to favor Moscow."

"Don't forget that your own side is conflicted. Corrupt US businessmen and officials are colluding with Putin, fueling and policing this war at the same time," Alexander concluded.

"I agree with you," said James.

Turning to Tatyana again, he continued, "At Belbek, next to the gate, I actually thought they were trying to kidnap you. Luckily, Alexander's reaction—and my own intuition—made me realize it was a personal matter. The Center confirmed your identities using the video I captured at that time and, of course, your fingerprints," he added, nodding in Alexander's direction.

"His fingerprints?" Tatyana asked.

A slight smile slipped over Alexander's lips. "I left them on his ID card."

Alexander gestured to the space around them and then directed a question at Robert, who had been sitting quietly, listening to the conversation. "Is this one of the Center's residences?" he asked.

Just then, the older woman who had answered the door shuffled in with coffee and cookies for everyone.

"Let's just call it my office," Robert replied.

As soon as she left, Robert spoke again.

"How did you hear the name Bill Brown?"

Alexander poured everyone coffee. "Someone did a poor job of erasing your real name and job number from the back of a folder."

Bill, or Robert as was his field identity, nodded and fell silent again. Alexander understood that he did not want to get his hands dirty in this situation, so he turned his attention back to James. But he knew that he had won some respect in unmasking the CIA operative.

"Having someone from Tatyana's circle in our organization has been a great asset. They're pushing me to have her help with some articles for my assignment overseas," Alexander continued.

"Am I being recruited?" Tatyana asked, nearly spilling her coffee.

"No, no," Alexander said reassuringly. "I mean simply what we discussed earlier."

He sipped his coffee and took a deep breath before placing the cup in its saucer. "I have been working with the Russian intelligence for a long time, protecting our mother country from infiltrators like Robert and James. But the events in Crimea…"

Alexander's eyes drifted to the window for a split second, his jaw hardening as he relived everything that he had seen. "I just witnessed the death of an innocent woman, full of life with her daughter and carrying a second child, brutally shot down at the hands of terrorists—sponsored by my own bosses."

He recounted everything that had happened in the Donetsk suburb. Demon, the businessman, the mysterious shot that had saved his life, the end of the Brotherhood. No one said a word while he recounted his tale. When he finished, a heavy silence hung in the air.

Tatyana placed her hand over his, tears in her eyes. "Thank you for what you did for her, for those people. You are truly brave." She exhaled loudly, wiped her tears swiftly with a napkin, and looked up at the men around the table. "So what do you need me to do? I don't know what kinds of stories would interest a Western reader in what is going on here. Maybe the Snowden scandals?"

"No," James said flatly. "We knew about Snowden's anti-American views years ago and gave him access to what he was interested in. We paid attention to which journalists were receiving the information of course. But we would prefer not to perpetuate the idea that he was some kind of martyr."

"Excuse the question, but why would you give him access at all? Why not throw him in jail?" asked Tatyana.

"We needed to follow the trail and see if the Chinese or the Russians were buying up secrets and who would go for the bait first. The Chinese turned out to be more cautious. Putin on the other hand, his ambition blurred his logic. As soon as the Russians downloaded Snowden's secret files, our program kicked into action and collected thousands of pages from the FSB and GRU. Now they're trying to keep this failure under wraps by holding Snowden up as a modern-day hero."

"Very clever," Alexander said. But in the back of his mind, he knew that there must be more to this story. James would not be so open as to tell him the full and complete truth just like that.

"Eventually, all of this will be made public," James continued. "But not right now. If you were to publicize this information," he said, turned towards Tatyana with a meaningful look in his eyes, "the Russian FSB or GRU would be knocking on your door asking how you got this information."

"So what do I do?" Tatyana asked, unfazed by James' veiled threat.

Alexander leaned over to grasp both of her hands in his.

James looked at Alexander and Tatyana and quietly said: "In a few days, Sharon, one of our 'journalists' will be in Siberia, in Novosibirsk, to cover some open court proceedings of Russian intellects, charges of espionage and corruption. We believe that topic will be interesting to American audiences."

She shook her head. "But I don't have the credentials to work there. And how can I write anything when my English is so unconvincing?"

"Don't worry about it, Tatyana. You will be excellent team with Sharon. Trust me."

"I fly to Moscow in a few hours to meet with General Malinkov," Alexander said. "I'll ask him to take care of your credentials."

James interrupted him. "Before you go on, I might be able to offer you some help with your General. Six months ago, his wife passed away from kidney cancer. The Kremlin denied his request to seek treatment for her in Germany. Not long after his wife died, his daughter—a doctor—and her husband—a prominent nuclear physicist—scheduled a visit to the United States. While getting their tourist visas at the embassy, they hinted at possibly working in America permanently. We do not believe the father was privy to this."

James rubbed the stubble on his cheek, and looked at each person seated around the table. "Considering time and the circumstances, we don't know if we'll ever have another opportunity like this to extend an offer to the General."

Then angrily, James added, "The Kremlin's hallucinations about restoring the 'great' Russian Empire won't bring the people anything but problems, tragedy, and discouragement. And this is just the start…only a rehearsal for what is yet to come." James did have Ukrainian blood after all.

Alexander nodded. "What do you think I should offer him, specifically?"

James considered the question for a moment. He looked towards Bill as if asking silently for his opinion. Bill nodded discretely.

"We are interested in everything related to hybrid wars and terrorist actions of the Russian Special Forces in our allied countries. That includes numbers, locations, contacts, weapons, plans, and times. We've heard unconfirmed rumors about an armed coup being organized in Russia."

"If that happens, we don't know what the consequences might be," James concluding, delivering his final statement directly to Alexander.

CHAPTER 11

The rest of the conversation back in Kiev had been logistical. Alexander left shortly thereafter for Moscow, on his way to see the General. The day was grey and wet, like so many in the capital. The taxi stopped near the Aquarium, the GRU headquarters, nicknamed for its overly modern, bulletproof glass structure. Alexander walked into the General's office at precisely 9:00 AM.

The General was seated behind a massive wooden desk, staring intently at his computer screen, which was angled purposely away from the eyes of any visitors. He clicked a few times to close whatever he was reviewing, likely related to the recent cyberattacks on Ukraine's power grid, and looking up calmly at Alexander.

"Well, Colonel Ivanov, I've heard quite a lot about you. You have made a good choice with your plan to travel to the US as a Russian Orthodox priest—this is a role that you could play very well, I believe."

Alexander felt a pang of regret, although he did not allow his emotion to show. For the government, religion was just a tool for manipulating the people. Putin's nationalism mixed well with the conservatism of the Orthodox Church, and he gained recognition as a savior for the believers oppressed under communism. But to mock the idea of true faith…Alex remembered the priest in Donetsk.

"Sir, I have credentials and some connections ready to pose as a journalist, I believe this would generate much more mobility."

The General studied Alexander and did not respond.

"My fiancé is in a position to write the necessary stories. She will work only with me and will not step outside the boundaries of her current job."

"Can we trust her? She's Ukrainian, is she not?"

It wasn't an unexpected question. "She is a good woman, strong, but obedient" said Alexander, imagining how Tatyana would react if she could hear him now. "We plan on getting married soon and living many years together, like you and your wife." Alexander softened his voice. "My condolences on her passing."

Alexander removed a piece of paper from his pocket. On it was scribbled "*Americans told me of daughter's plans, can we meet at Gorky Park tonight?*" He handed it to the General.

The General silently read the paper, then looked up at Alexander again with expressionless eyes. Alexander understood that he needed to take the first step for the General to trust him and to prove that this was not a setup.

"I am sure General, that Tatyana will not disappoint you. Also, Comrade General, out of respect, in my rank, I am only a Lieutenant Colonel…"

Alexander paused before continuing, and the General interjected. "Until today you were a Lieutenant Colonel, but now you are a Colonel. So, let us toast to your beautiful fiancée, and celebrate your promotion Comrade Colonel. How about this evening—seven? At Gorky Park?"

So far, so good, Alexander thought as he smiled back.

Gorky Park

Alexander missed the old Gorky Park. When was younger, there had been rides and games—Ferris wheels, rollercoasters, and countless other ways in which the young and old alike could enjoy themselves. The rides were demolished years ago, and though the new, green expanse was certainly calming, he couldn't help but wish for the noise of all those families. Alexander walked up to the park gates exactly at seven. The General was already there, unsurprisingly.

They strolled through the park, talking about mundane matters such as the brisk evening weather and the unbearable traffic. They came to a small bar with twinkling lights decorating the dark interior. The General ordered a bottle of Burgundy for the table, "to drink for the bride and groom."

After the waiter poured their glasses, Alexander brought up Tatyana's trip to Siberia. "Right now in Novosibirsk there are ongoing court proceedings that involve a group of scientists. Tatyana familiarized herself with some of the cases as best she could. She says that the material could be very interesting for Western audiences. She just needs the access to put it together."

"My son-in-law is a nuclear physicist. In their circles, they say that to be labeled an intellect is to be a future prisoner; you either go to prison, or the prison comes after you. She will receive the credentials tomorrow morning, but all materials must be approved by us before publication."

They finished their wine slowly, as if they had all the time in the world. Afterwards, they left the bar and meandered toward a trail in a somewhat less crowded area. Finally, when Alexander was convinced they would not be overheard, he broached the true subject of the meeting.

He turned to face the General. "Comrade General, the Americans believe your daughter and son-in-law are interested in working in the States. Permanently. Obviously, the Americans would appreciate your understanding and your help."

The General frowned and did not answer right away. Alexander followed his lead and they walked deeper into the park. They walked for several more minutes in silence, each step making Alexander's heart race in fear. Had he been mistaken? If he had been tricked and was going to meet an untimely end, this was certainly the place for it to happen. He clenched his fists, prepared to battle to the end.

Finally, the General spoke quietly, without looking at Alexander. "The printing house in Donetsk. Your work or that of the Right Sector?"

"Mine. Those weren't even people anymore," Alexander answered just as quietly.

"Very clean. We believed it was the Right Sector. May it remain that way."

Alexander was relieved, but the recruitment was not a success. Not yet.

"There's never money for medicine," the General said, his voice still hushed. "And if there is, then you can't get the medicine or travel for the cancer treatment. Instead, our officials use the most effective nine-gram lead pill. Do you know how many have committed suicide? One shot and no more pain or anger—not at the government, not at the oligarchs, just eternal peace. My daughter was raised in the spirit of patriotism. However, when her mother was denied by our government to get cancer treatment in Germany or the US and died as a result, my daughter was changed. She knows very well that our government and oligarchs treat their animals much better than own people. She told me her decision to leave Russia for the USA. I didn't blame her for that. It was done with my approval. I sacrificed the life of my wife for the sake of my country. I am ready to sacrifice my career, but not the future of my daughter."

Alexander didn't know what to say, so he said nothing.

"What do our colleagues want?" the General finally asked.

"They are concerned about weapons of mass destruction getting onto the black market. Rumors of a coup in Russia are circulating, and they want to know about possible hot spots. They also want counts and locations of Russian operatives interfering with the American political process and names of their domestic allies."

"Set up a meeting in Vladivostok. Let's call it 'Expanding the Far East Economy.'" The General chuckled dryly. "Meet the conditions of American sanctions to justify its secretiveness. Have someone at the meeting who can guarantee its impact at the executive level in America. We'll discuss the terrorist groups at the meeting. Neutralizing some will not solve the problem; new ones are always ready to take their place." He turned and held out a hand to Alexander. "You've got two weeks to set it up."

Before Alexander could respond, the General disappeared into the blackness of the trees.

～CHAPTER 12～

Vladivostok

At 11:30 in the early afternoon, a group of American business-men—four men and one woman, a specialist in Russian natural resources—arrived in Vladivostok. As soon as they passed through customs, a middle-aged woman in fur-lined boots with a matching coat flagged them down and escorted them to the hotel.

Their guide, Galina Petrova, told them to meet in the lobby at 5 PM and she would take them to the restaurant for dinner. When they arrived, they found the restaurant's tables were covered with white cloths and all sorts of local delicacies; black caviar and scallops with wild garlic. Galina ushered the Americans to a table where three people were already waiting: Alexander, General Ma-linkov, and one of the most successful businessmen of Primorsky Krai, Yuri Tretyakov.

Alexander immediately stood and shook the Americans' hands, lingering on James a little longer. He was glad that James was able to be part of the group. The evening was lively, joyful, and interesting. The Americans shared their first impressions of the Primorsky Territory, and Yuri, in turn, told interesting stories about hunting, fishing, and—of course—the beauty and richness of his native land. Not a word was said about the business, although everyone was silently evaluating the situation.

At the end of the meal, Yuri invited everyone to visit his vacation house the following day, promising kebobs, fried fish, and even some hunting. The others readily agreed, and the next day around noon, a van with tinted windows entered Yuri's country home. Alexander, Yuri, and the General all welcomed the Americans.

"Welcome, dear guests," Yuri said. "Now before we head inside for a little business, let me reassure you that the General and his men—as well as my own—have checked this area and the house repeatedly." He stressed the last word, and everyone offered a polite laugh.

Once inside the home's expansive living room, the Americans introduced themselves once again, and Yuri introduced his business companions in attendance. The General introduced Roman Orlov, Mark Cheremushkin, and Ruslan Kornilov—members of the management committee forming new, independent governments in the territories of modern Russia. The Americans included Emily, an expert on Russia who spoke Russian and often whispered translations to her companions, as well as Terry Inmen, one of the president's advisers for issues pertaining to Russia. Two security personnel tagged along as well.

The General started the meeting. "We are here today to decide the fate of Russia. The purpose of our meeting is not to divide this great land, but to save the Slavic people and the world from a nuclear catastrophe. In recent years, beginning with the annexation of Crimea—an undeclared war with Ukraine—and the intimidation of the Americans to turn the United States and its allies into radioactive ashes, our country has become a nuclear scarecrow trying to intimidate the civilized world."

He approached a section of the wall closed off by curtains and pressed a button on a nearby remote control. The curtains parted to reveal a monitor displaying two maps.

"On the left side," the General motioned with the remote in his hand, "you see the modern Russia with its strategic objects ready to turn America into ashes at any second, alongside any number of other enemies." He gestured generally around the map, not calling out any specific aggressor, but demonstrating that the Russian government was prepared to disregard any allegiances. On the right side, you see the potential borders of independent countries in the territory of modern Russia."

His words were stern and forceful, and he had the rapt attention of his audience. The General continued. "Unfortunately, since the times of Kuzka's mother, we have still not been able to offer the civilized world anything other than these nuclear horror stories."

"Excuse me," Emily interrupted. "'Kuzka's mother'?"

The General smiled good-naturedly. "The young generation missed so much in the infamous sixties. It is a Russian saying, meaning that we will punish you. In 1960, during a speech at the UN, Nikita Khrushchev used this expression to address the Western world—the United States, in particular. 'We will catch up and surpass, we shall show you Kuzka's mother.'" The General chuckled at the memory.

"Not even the translators knew what he was talking about. In those times, even in the governing circles of the former USSR, only a very few amount of people knew the real meaning of 'Kuzka's mother.' But a year later, everyone knew what it meant after our TU-95B bomber dropped the mother over the New World test site.

The General continued, clearly enjoying the shock creeping onto the Americans' faces. There was a reason that he had signed up for government service.

"The fifty-megaton bomb made the whole planet shiver. The temperature at the epicenter of the explosion was so high that the stones turned to ashes. The explosion wave circled the Earth several times. Its impact was felt thousands of kilometers away. Suddenly, the threshold of biblical Armageddon became a reality—a threshold that is relentlessly approaching us today. Some of the projects were stopped for their inhuman nature or because the technology needed more time to develop—but today, many of them are being resurrected."

"And how many of these weapons are at the disposal of the new regime?'" Terry asked. "What compels Putin to show off his nuclear weapons? Russia is well aware that, even without NATO, the United States' capabilities are far superior. We have never threatened you with atomic bombs, even when you didn't have them yet. We even tried to help you out of your crisis."

"Putin and his administration know full well that you are not planning to attack us," the General said. He tapped the table with a finger. "That is not what he is afraid of."

"Then what is he afraid of?" Emily asked.

"Losing power. He sees Russia as his own possession."

"And the people put up with it all," Emily concluded, shaking her head.

"The people of Russia don't see their squalid conditions, dying of state-sponsored hunger in villages, no work to keep the men from drinking. They consider themselves happy and almighty, ready to defend their motherland from capitalist interventionists at a moment's notice," the General said.

"The Russian propaganda machine is truly an unsurpassable art form," Terry said.

"And now the Kremlin has used its skills to paint Putin as a hero and a savior of the common man," Yuri added. This was dangerous, as well as ironic, given that he had amassed a fortune funneling public money through back door contracts. But Yuri had seen enough suffering, and also, his position was not as secure as it once had been.

"The Kremlin can also use its army to promote its ideals in the most unforeseen areas," the General went on, looking at Alexander. "Our country is experiencing Putinization, and everything will depend on loyalty to Putin. Even our religions are not based on the dogmatic principles of faith, but on how to be a patriot, who to believe in. No one even remembers the separation of church and state under the Soviets. The church is wholly serving the government, and we will soon have millions of active religious fanatics ready to fulfill any request made by the monarch of Russia, in any part of the world. We perfectly understand that we cannot win a nuclear war. But we can conquer the Western world through propaganda."

"Sounds like Putinism will be much harder to defeat than Communism," Dan suggested.

"My friend, that is the understatement of the century," the general offered. "The Soviets persecuted our many immigrant peoples for decades, locking then in prison for years. Today these same persecuted individuals—and their families—see Putin as a real world leader and Russia as an undefeated empire."

He shook his head. "And you are playing right into his hands. The Kremlin is making a huge bet on the resources of your mass media. You would not believe how many wealthy and influential people already offer their services to us, blind to the horrors waiting for them."

Emily interrupted. "What do you mean, blind to the horrors?"

"For example," the General said, spreading his heads, "one very successful Russian in Crimea owned all the bus stations on the Crimean peninsula. He supported Russia's accession of Crimea, investing many of his own resources into the idea. When Russian troops arrived in Crimea, he was overjoyed—until a couple of weeks when they threw him out of his office and nationalized his business."

Yuri and the other businessmen nodded somberly. The General sighed heavily before continuing.

"Make no mistake. Putin and the Kremlin will enact laws against his opponents while rewarding his supporters with more freedom. Your mass media resources will play their role, but we can also use hybrid wars and display our special military operations if need be. We will deprive the West of the opportunity to engage in an open war with us because the army of the 'Russian world' will be blocking all key positions of its authority. The development and execution of these operations is a general's duty. But in this case, a large portion of the task is on the shoulders of a young, but experienced and talented, colonel of Russian's foreign intelligence. This man, Alexander Denisovich Ivanov." The General placed his hand on Alexander's shoulders.

The guests all turned toward him. Alexander nodded his head respectfully in return. His heart pumping and heat rising in his cheeks, Alexander hoped that he did not seem visibly nervous.

"We understand that the Kremlin is playing with fire," the General continued. "Russia has already stepped over the line of a cold war. Not all of Putin's 'war games' can go as planned. Their exodus and our destinies will be unpredictable, which is why we want to apply maximum diligence and not give even a small chance for Putin's Armageddon to be unleashed."

Alexander spoke up, completing the General's thought. "Putin lost his chance to resign with dignity. He understands that now, in the best case scenario, a tribunal is awaiting him. What kind? I don't know. Maybe an all-Russian one, maybe an all-nation one. He knows that wars, military conflicts and intrigues where Russia is constantly 'surrounded by damned Western occupiers' can keep him at the helm—not to mention breathing life into that old promise to fulfill Stalin and Mao Tse-tung's dream of a unified Russia and China." Alexander looked at the General.

The General seemed pleased. "But he understands that if Russia has to switch roles, from the older brother to the younger brother of the Chinese nation, he will quickly turn from a younger brother into an enemy of the nation."

"And the fate of such people is solved quickly in China," Terry said. "China will simply swallow Russia whole. It's certainly big enough, and they have not made the same economic mistakes."

The General nodded. "But none of us wants to be the hostages of the whims and ambitions of a political maniac like Putin."

"What are you proposing moving forward?" Terry asked.

The General pointed to Roman, Mark, and Ruslan. "At a recent meeting, the decision was made to establish three independent states: the DNR or Far East People's Republic, the FRS or Federative Republic of Siberia, and the Federative Republic of Kuban. They will be open to diplomatic solutions with the West. We would like to offer the Western countries a project to create a small, neutral government on the territory of Konigsberg (Kaliningrad) —a kind of Switzerland on the Baltic Sea."

The members of the American delegation exchanged wary looks. Finally, Terry spoke.

"We understand the unfolding situation and will advise our government to react with understanding to your peaceful intentions. But it is very hard to believe that Putin will agree to a peaceful option. What happens if he decides to apply force instead? We are especially concerned about each side's nuclear arsenal. Nobody can foresee the chances of using them and at what scale."

"Russian civil war is inevitable," Alexander said quietly.

They all knew this to be true, but no one had wanted to say it. The room went quiet. Now that the likelihood of civil war had been mentioned, the tone of the conversation shifted. As a heavy silence fell over the room, everyone considered the implications of Alexander's statement.

"The war with Ukraine solidified our future," the General finally said. "Putin will not stop at Ukraine. He wants to provoke NATO and European countries against each other. Military conflicts will ensue. He has footholds in Belarus, and has planned significant war games in the coming months.

"But when coffins with Russian men from around the world begin arriving in Russia, the nation will explode. Russians can tolerate hunger and cold, but not death knocking on their doorstep. The atrocities of World War II endured in our motherland still run deep in our memories."

"Putin recently enacted a law about the confidentiality of statistical data about fallen soldiers and officers," Alexander pointed out. "If he was planning a peaceful coexistence, there would be no need for such a law. He sees what is coming, and is preparing to hide the facts from the Russian people."

"A civil war will be chaotic, bloody, and fruitless," Nikolay interjected. "But even if our relationship with the Kremlin grows into a military conflict, we guarantee full control of the arms that are at our disposal in our newly established states. Moscow's military potential will be limited. It will not be able to carry out military action on all fronts, both within Russia and outside of it."

The General stood, and began to slowly pace up and down the length of the largest bookshelf. "And Russia's satellites, such as Belarus, will not lose their chance to escape from Moscow's circle of control. This will destabilize the Kremlin's position even further," he said.

"Will the United States or NATO take part in any of these military actions? Many of the players here are not members of NATO," Emily said. "If you can solve this problem in a peaceful manner, we will have many more opportunities to help each of your countries."

"We already have several influential people in Putin's inner circle," Roman said.

"And the FSB's position?" Emily asked pointedly.

"One of elite authority, as always," the General said, sitting back down. "They have the glory and the privilege and the money. They look at the armed forces with open contempt, as a lower class."

"And in terms of their loyalty to Putin?" Emily asked. Alexander hid a smile. He admired her shrewdness and to-the-point approach.

"Agitation is bubbling among them as well," the General said. "Not all of them want to circle around Putin forever. But no matter what kind of adherent to Putin you are, and no matter how many privileges you may have, over time you understand that the greatest privilege is freedom. The majority of them well understand that the tougher your sanctions are the fewer chances they have for freedom—the fewer chances they have to be themselves. We don't know how much longer their patience will last. However, while the devil may joke around, we prefer to keep a distance from them. We limit ourselves to working relationships."

"What do you expect from us and our allies?" Terry asked. "How can we be useful?"

"Acknowledgement of our countries, removal of the sanctions, and the establishment of friendly political, economic, and cultural relationships," Ruslan said. "We want to become a part of the civilized world and see our people happy—not when they have a bottle in their hand and the television is promising to turn the damned USA into radioactive ash, but when their stomachs are full and their minds are sober. When a mother doesn't have to think about what to prepare for dinner for her child. When a father isn't thinking about where to borrow money from in order to feed his family or to pay off their debt. When everyone can be themselves and speak their minds without any fear. We would like to visit you and wish for you to be welcome in our homes."

"You helped Germany and Japan rise from the ruins of the Second World War," Roman said. "They became advanced countries. We are counting on tight cooperation with you in all spheres."

"And of course to keep peace on our planet," the General added. "In a world with such men and weapons, the world's very survival must be paramount. In the worst case scenario, if Russia has no future, then no one can rest safely in their beds. Wild instincts prevail over strong minds."

"Can the oligarchs force Putin to make a peaceful transition of authority?" Terry asked.

The General interlaced his fingers and considered his words carefully before speaking. "Putin noted one his predecessor's mistakes—namely, that of Lavrentiy Beria. After Stalin's death, Beria insufficiently surrounded himself with Special Services. He didn't have time to establish control over the armed forces. Much like the Army does not get along with the KGB today. Khrushchev used this moment to his advantage and arrested Beria, charging him with anti-party and anti-government activity. Beria's fate had been decided even before his arrest. Khrushchev knew that if Beria remained alive and came to power, the streets would run red with blood."

"Perhaps so, but if Beria was ready to fill the streets of the Soviet Union with blood, then Khrushchev was ready to turn the whole Western world into radioactive ash long before Putin," Emily pointed out.

"Precisely my point," the general said, bowing slightly to her. "Putin noted Beria's mistake and surrounded himself with a hand-crafted Special Services apparatus and a limited number of oligarchs. And unlike the Soviet politburo, Putin's oligarchs not only have a certain level of authority, but they also have a minimum level of capital—billions of dollars, in fact. Putin and his circle are completely dependent upon each other. Even if one knocks Putin out of the way to become the new president of Russia, absolutely nothing will change. A new president from the same club? However, he does have one trick that he might deploy."

"Which is?" Teri inquired quietly.

It is very possible that he will be able to make one of his daughters the president. But of course, everyone will understand that he will remain in the control of all Russia. It will be like changing the position of terms in an equation: The result doesn't change."

"We were under the Mongol-Tatar shadow for far too long to be able to think in a European manner," Yuri said. "Too much Mongol-Tatar blood flows through our veins for feelings of democracy to become our natural qualities and to make principles of democratic rule our reality. Whomever we put to rule in Russia, that person will always think that only they can exist forever—and of course, that they are everywhere and that there should be no boundaries to Russia's empire."

"But my colleagues," Yuri continued, "I do not want to continue this kind of politics. Seventy years ago we destroyed Germany, taking almost all of her riches, intellect, and scientists, but today we are the ones begging Germany for money."

"Even Japan quickly rose from the horror of its nuclear destruction and became a leading country in the world," Roman added. "We want that kind of revival."

The General stood again and paced in front of the others, then stopped and held out his hands. "I was a sincere communist. I built this government. But, I never imagined what that it would come to this—we thought we were building paradise, but we laid the bricks of hell instead. We spoke of a bright future, but arrived at a hopeless present. I will use my influence and experience to help our new government find people whom Siberia can trust and whom you will be able to trust in your nation, my American colleagues. I only hope for your government's understanding and support."

CHAPTER 13

<u>Novosibirsk</u>

Tatyana was in a pensive mood. She was set to fly out to
Siberia soon, but first she stopped by the editing house to grab a
few things. She busied herself for a few moments, opening filing
cabinets and pulling papers out. She grabbed an extra recorder,
some paperclips. *What else?* she thought. Her activity was interrupted by a sudden knock at her open door.

"Look at what these Moskals are saying about Ukrainians,"
her friend Zina said, flowing into the office. She was younger than
Tatyana, with very long hair. Tatyana always felt she was quick to
righteous anger—an admirable trait in a journalist. Zina held a
stack of Russian newspapers, which she unceremoniously threw on
the table. "The bastards were quiet all these years, called themselves

the brotherly nation, and now overnight these brotherly people turned into fascists. Idiots!"

Tatyana shook her head. "Don't take it so seriously, Zina. I promise to bring you a lot of interesting material from Siberia." She truly hoped to deliver on that promise.

"That will be nice," Zina said wistfully. "Nothing sooths the soul like a juicy story to print. I thought your plane was leaving in a couple of hours? You should get going."

"I am," Tatyana replied as she stood up and put on her jacket. "See you on the other side."

And just like that, Tatyana was on her way.

Sharon was the first to arrive in Novosibirsk Tolmachevo Airport. She was wearing a suit, something she was not used to. *Spies should dress for comfort,* she thought to herself irritably. She glanced at her watch, and decided that she would grab something to eat while she waited for Tatyana's plane. She soon found a small vendor selling belyashi, and she took up her post.

While waiting for Tatyana's plane to arrive, she noticed a crowd of people through the airport's windows. They were holding posters that said, "Hand off 'Free Siberia' Radio." An idea formulated in her mind.

When Tatyana landed, Sharon quickly introduced herself. She had gotten some information on the fiery Ukrainian journalist, and after exchanging a few pleasantries she decided to get right down to business. As the two began leaving the airport, she pointed to the protesters through the window. "I'm thinking there are probably some radio people right outside the airport here who can give us a head start on finding out the real scoop on the judicial proceedings. You're game to give it a shot, right?"

"Absolutely," Tatyana said, her journalistic fire sparking to life at the challenge. She checked to make sure she had a pen and paper handy, as well as her trusted recorder. Good thing she brought two. "Let's do it!"

A few minutes later, they walked outside and were hit by the bracingly cold air of the Siberian tundra. It took a minute to acclimate to the cold, but soon enough Tatyana was in good form, firing off questions in every direction. They asked the protesters if any radio people were among them, and an energetic young girl led them to a man named Igor. He was the Director of the radio station and had, it turned out, been following the proceedings with great interest. Igor was more than happy to meet a journalist from the former Soviet Republic, but when he found out that Sharon was an American journalist, she became like a small window into the world of freedom.

"I will try to do anything I can for you," Igor said. "But I want to warn you from the beginning that, behind all this stands a large, authoritative Kremlin machine."

"Why do you think so?" Sharon asked.

"I don't think so, I *know* so. I have my own, good connections with the big governmental circles of Siberia. They love our radio show and truly want to see Siberia free from Moscow's horde. They are tired of stealing from their own people to send tribute to Kremlin's magnates. You know what they told me when I turned to them for help?"

"What?" Tatyana asked, pen poised in the air theatrically.

"'We love you, we love your people and all that you are doing. But don't come here, don't call us. Lay low. Your time will come.'"

Sharon motioned to the protesters. "This is what you call laying low?"

Igor laughed. "The Kremlin cannot make all of Siberia stay low. She has been there far too long already."

"So you've been following the judicial proceedings?" Tatyana asked.

"Damn Kremlin is setting up our scientists and nobody knows why. They let Usachev go free yesterday, but warned him not to leave Novosibirsk."

A police officer approached Igor and whispered in his ear. Igor nodded and then called out the protesters. "That's it for today, people. Wrap it up."

"Police trouble?" Sharon asked.

Igor shook his head. "Foreigners flying in. FSB is already on its way. Our authorities want everything quiet when they arrive." He eyed the women closely, as if suddenly realizing that they could be the foreigners the FSB was looking for.

"Say, Igor, do you think you can help us meet with Usachev?" Sharon asked quickly, trying to distract him. "Maybe even right now, if you're not busy? The news waits for no one."

"We just need to see him personally and confirm that he is alive and well," Tatyana added quickly.

Igor smiled at them with admiration. "You journalists are cleverer than our FSB. Let's go." He motioned to the taxi stand.

"Uh, maybe a bus instead?" Sharon asked.

Tatyana leaned closer to Sharon and whispered, "What's wrong with a taxi?"

"The first thing the FSB will do is question the taxi drivers," Sharon hissed.

Tatyana nodded in agreement, then called out to Igor, "How about a private car?"

Sharon held out money to him, but Igor held up his hands to warn her off. "You're my guests. I'll take care of it."

Sharon shoved the money in Igor's pocket unceremoniously. "When your radio station is working again, then you can take care of it."

Twenty minutes later, they were pulling up to a five-story building. It was a relic of the Soviet era, a heavy concrete block with too-small windows. Sharon and Tatyana exited the car while Igor paid the driver. Sharon whispered to Tatyana, "Follow my lead."

To Igor, she said, "Let's not overwhelm Usachev with all our excitement. You and Tatyana take a stroll around the driveway to the building and I will I run up to speak to him. If anything out of the ordinary happens down here, call me on my cellphone, okay?"

"Sounds good," Tatyana said. "I'd like to stretch my legs after the plane ride anyway."

Igor shrugged. "No problem. It's apartment thirty—on the third floor."

Halfway up the stairs, Sharon paused. She took a quick glance over the railing. She appeared to be alone in the stairwell. Hurriedly she pulled out a scrap of paper from her brief, and on it wrote, "Greetings to you from your friend from Moscow." If the FSB knew about her arrival, then Usachev's unexpected release from prison could be connected to her. The apartment could be under audio and video surveillance.

At his door, she started to ring the doorbell, but changed her mind. Quietly she knocked on the door instead.

"Who's there?" a man's voice called from the other side.

"It's me."

"Who's me?"

"I have a letter for you."

The door opened to reveal a casually dressed man. He was thin and pale. To Sharon, he certainly looked the part of downtrodden Russian scientist.

"Are you Victor Abramovich Usachev?" she asked politely.

"Yes, and you are?"

Sharon held up the piece of paper for him to read and placed a finger over her mouth. "I was asked to pass a letter on to you."

He looked at her attentively, then hesitantly stepped aside and motioned her into the hallway.

"I'm in bit of a hurry," Sharon said. "Would you mind walking me out?" She motioned purposefully towards the stairwell with a tilt of her head.

Halfway down the stairs, where they had an unobstructed view of everything above and below them, they stopped. Sharon leaned close and whispered who she was. "Your friend from Moscow told me that you have some interesting inventions for us, which you'd like to pass on to him. Unfortunately, the connection was lost."

Clearly unused to espionage, Usachev leaned in, and in an even quieter whisper, said, "Yes, I was determining the fate of strategic rockets, submarines, and planes. But when I found out that I was being watched, I destroyed all the equipment and burned the calculations. All that is left is what's in my head."

"I see," Sharon said, trying to figure out how to proceed from here. Not having any documentation was a setback.

"But you might be interested in what I found out from Professor Mosin while in prison. He's a chemist."

Sharon recognized the name. "His trial scheduled in a couple of days, right?"

Usachev nodded. "He knows what the Kremlin is planning."

"And what is that?"

Usachev shrugged. "We were separated before he could say. Find a way to meet with him. He's more important to you now than my project. Meanwhile, I'll try to rebuild what I can, now that I know I have friendly eyes on me." They heard voices then. Usachev started back up the stairs. "Send greetings to my friend. I have not forgotten about him."

Sharon remained silent for most of drive to the hotel, thinking about the situation with Usachev and Mosin. When they arrived, she invited Igor to lunch with them. They sat at a small table in the corner of the hotel restaurant. Sharon asked the waiter to remove the vase of flowers, blaming it on allergies. She knew how well such flowers could pay attention to the conversations of foreign visitors. She took out her mirror and lipstick. Then she slowly opened lipstick, examined herself in the mirror and, as if deciding not to make up her lips, closed the container quickly with a tap to its cover. The distortion device was now turned on. They could talk freely without the risk of being recorded.

"Do you have any kind of connection with the prison, the investigators, or the prosecutor's office?" Sharon asked Igor. "We'd really like to meet with Professor Mosin before the trial."

Igor nodded slowly. "It won't be cheap, though."

"Money isn't an issue." She gave him her cell phone number.

They spent the rest of the meal talking about the power of honest journalism with Igor, wowing him with abridged and slightly altered versions of their true experiences. After all, they hesitated to trust him completely, but needed to earn his respect and friendship. By the end of the meal, Sharon was convinced that Igor would do what they asked. She shot Tatyana a glance that said, "We make a good team, don't we?"

Igor excused himself eventually, and the two women checked in to their hotel room. After showering and finally changing out of their travel clothes, Tatyana and Sharon took up posts in the room. Tatyana listened to the recordings she had made, making sure that the audio was clear, and Sharon sat patiently, running the events of the day through her head. A few hours later, Igor called Sharon to tell her everything was set up. She cut him off and told him to come to the hotel. When Igor arrived fifteen minutes later, Sharon was already waiting for him at the entrance, after telling Tatyana to stay put for the meantime.

"Let's take a little walk and you can share your news," she said to Igor.

"The deal is set with an investigator. He will be questioning Mosin tomorrow—not in prison, but in his office. They are transporting him tomorrow at 11:00 AM. The car will stop in this spot." He pulled out a small map and pointed to an intersection circled in pen. "Security will leave him unattended in the police wagon, and the front passenger door will be unlocked. You should not have to deal with anyone, but you will have no more than five minutes. It will cost you three thousand dollars—and only one of you can speak with him."

"First the merchandise, so to speak, and then the money."

Igor nodded. "I figured. I gave myself up as a guarantee. Don't let me down." He pulled his phone out of his pocket. "I downloaded his photo to show you."

To maintain the ruse, she glanced at the photograph. "Thank you, Igor." Of course, she knew what he looked like already.

After she saw him off in a taxi, Sharon walked further down the street, away from the hotel, until she found a telephone booth next to a bus station. She entered the booth, closed the door tightly, dialed a number, said something short, and hung up. Then she waited. A few minutes later, the phone rang. Sharon answered.

"I need a taxi for two to three hours tomorrow. I have a meeting with a client. I'll be waiting for you next to the hotel at ten. Thank you."

Returning to the hotel, Sharon told Tatyana that she would be going to the meeting on her own.

Tatyana was skeptical. "You do realize you could enter a police wagon and come out of it far, far away?"

"You're absolutely right, but I believe in the power of the American dollar more than in their honesty and justice. Let's hope for the best, but be prepared for the worst," Sharon said, which seemed to relax Tatyana a bit. "If you don't hear from me by five tomorrow evening, take this envelope. There's money for unforeseen expenses and a telephone number. Call it and tell whoever answers that Sharon sends her greetings. Tell them the trial was delayed indefinitely and you're returning to Kiev. Then fly out immediately. Someone will meet you in Kiev. Tell them everything you know."

Tatyana remained dubious, but ultimately took the envelope from Sharon.

At 10:00 the next morning, a black Volga with tinted windows drove up to the hotel. Sharon checked the number as she walked up to the car. A rather short driver jumped out of the car, politely opened the front door for Sharon, and just as politely closed it.

Two more people sat in the car. The driver sped away from the hotel, taking a circuitous route to the rendezvous point to check for tails.

"Everything set?" she asked with no introduction.

The man behind the passenger seat nodded. "We've been keeping the hotel under supervision for two hours already. We've got two transients in place. If the police try to kidnap you, they'll take care of you. The professor will have to stay. Our sources suggest it's a poison and the GRU is already on to it. We need to know what the poison is and who it's for." He had a full beard, and had kept his sunglasses on inside the car.

"And we're sure it's the professor being transported?" Sharon asked.

The other man, a heavyset type wearing a leather jacket, answered. "We've had the prison under watch. Mosin has been prepared for transport at the very least."

Sunglasses said, "After the operation, a white Volga will be waiting for you at the corner next to the café." He showed her a photo of the driver and the car's license plate number. "Got it memorized?"

"Yes. I need more money."

"The driver will give you ten thousand dollars and one hundred thousand rubles. He will also give you the code for a storage locker at the airport. You'll find more dollars and rubles there, if necessary," Jacket replied.

After circling the streets, the driver finally stopped at a café not far from the rendezvous point. Sharon exited the car, stopped at the café for a coffee and a newspaper, and made her way to the yard to wait for the police wagon.

She didn't have to wait long.

When the police wagon appeared, it pulled up near Sharon's perch. The driver cracked the window. "Journalist?"

She nodded.

The driver exited and walked around to the area where prisoners were kept. "I have to search you."

Sharon shrugged. "Don't get too excited," she said, handing him her purse. "My shade of lipstick is from last season."

"The purse stays with me," he said, unimpressed by her humor.

"That's mighty convenient, given the five thousand dollars inside." Sharon eyed the man carefully. "Tell you what, you hold on to the purse for me. I'll take my mirror and lipstick, if you don't mind." She plucked both items from the purse that he still held in his hands. "And for your troubles I'll give you...one hundred dollars."

"Make it two."

"For two can you guarantee no problems and no headaches?"

The driver held out his hand expectantly. She counted out two hundred dollars, which he quickly shoved into his pocket before knocking on the police wagon's door. The door swung open from within. Two security guards with AK-47 guns were sitting at the door. Behind them, separated by a wall of bars, was the prisoner.

"Your five minutes have already started," the driver said.

"Chop, chop," Sharon said to the guards. "Time for your smoke break."

"We are not allowed to leave you alone with the prisoner."

Sharon looked at the driver, clearly exasperated.

He smirked rudely before saying, "Perhaps a hundred dollars each will lighten their feet?"

"Of course!" The security guards answered just as rudely.

"Everyone is so hungry in Siberia." Sharon held out the bills, forcing the guards to exit before they could get paid. As they reached for the money, she slid through the door, pulling it closed behind her.

Sharon took a seat closer to the bars and looked at a prisoner. "Professor Mosin?"

"What do you want?" His voice was timid.

"I am an American journalist." Sharon opened her lipstick and closed it right away, slightly pressing a lit. "We can talk freely, I've blocked any listening devices, but we only have five minutes. Victor Abramovich Usachev told me you knew what the Kremlin was up to. A poison, right?"

He nodded slowly.

"What is the poison? Who are the targets?"

He furrowed his brow in frustration and disbelief. "Who are you really?"

"Like I said, a journalist. I'm covering your trial." On a thick layer of dust on the wall, she used her finger to write "CIA," then erased it thoroughly.

The professor moved closer to the bars to whisper at Sharon. "It is to be used against you and others."

"I need details: where, when, in what way?"

He shook his head, clearly frightened. "I don't care if they kill me, but they've threatened to kill my wife. I cannot risk her life."

"You've got to agree to continue working on this project."

"What?" the professor practically screeched with terror and shock, albeit keeping his voice low and hushed.

"They're already looking for your replacement. If they find someone, you will lose all value to them." She let the words sink in. "Continue working on the project and we will work with you, find some kind of antidote. Tell the investigator that you agree to this, and we will pay him to close the case."

The professor signaled for Sharon to move closer. Barely making a sound, he whispered, "The poison is ready, and the vaccine is almost ready. You alone know this. I will agree to this."

The next day, Professor Mosin found himself enjoying lunch with his wife in his own apartment. The entire affair had gone even easier than he could have hoped. Whatever agency was greasing the wheels behind the scene had done a good job. Just as the woman had said. When an American journalist called requesting an interview, he agreed immediately.

Sharon and Tatyana arrived in a rental car, just in time for tea. Things began innocuously. Sharon asked about the woodcarvings in the yard. The professor gave them a tour. Then Sharon asked Tatyana to snap a few pictures of the figurines for the press.

"We have to fly out tomorrow morning. It would be very good if we could take pictures of everything you have," said Sharon pointedly.

"The rest of my collection is about thirty kilometers from here."

Sharon smiled. "We can take our rental car."

The professor nodded at Tatyana, who was still snapping photos. "Is she also from your 'publishing house?'"

Sharon smiled widely. "No. She is a Ukrainian journalist. She'll write up a fabulous story based on the interview you gave us today." Sharon nodded in the direction of a grocery store she had spotted down the block. "Perhaps you need to grab some cigarettes?"

The professor nodded. Sharon and Tatyana said their goodbyes to his wife. Sharon drove around for fifteen minutes to check for tails before returning to the grocery store.

Tatyana said nothing, and Sharon was grateful that the other woman had learned not to ask any questions, even though it went against her nature as a journalist. She would do just fine as a spy, Sharon decided.

In the store, Sharon walked up to the professor and quietly told him to make his way out to the car through the back exit and sit in the backseat, where he would be less noticeable.

"Someone called as soon as you left the house," the professor said once they were on their way in the car.

This wasn't good news for Sharon. If counterintelligence began doubting the professor, they could still push to get everything out of him. But to abort such an important operation because of some unconfirmed facts went against her training. Sharon stepped on the gas.

They drove in silence, with only the professor occasionally speaking to give out the directions. Just as they entered the forest, Sharon's phone rang. She lifted it to her ear and kept driving.

"A jeep is moving in your direction, on another road. Our road is closed. An accident of some sort. Abort—repeat, abort."

She gritted her teeth. "Negative." She snapped the phone shut.

Tatyana raised a questioning eyebrow to Sharon, but said nothing. A moment later, she turned toward the professor. "It's beautiful here."

"Yes," the professor agreed, but he wasn't looking well. He offered a weak smile. "Sometimes I get a bit carsick." He removed his blazer and draped it over his knees. He closed his eyes and took several deep breaths. When he opened his eyes again, he noticed a small piece of plastic along the collar of his blazer. "What is this?"

He pulled it off and placed it on Tatyana's outstretched hand. She held it up for Sharon to see.

"Damn," Sharon said. "Were you wearing this blazer when they arrested you?"

The professor shook his head. "They took me from my apartment, in a shirt only."

"So they were either in your apartment or at the store." Sharon tapped the brakes. "We have to abort the operation."

"We're just about a kilometer away," the professor said. When the car continued to slow, he leaned forward over the front seat. "Hit the gas. I am already a dead man. I'll give you everything, all the originals. I'll stay behind and stall. Just don't return by this road. Go straight and in five kilometers, there is a big village and beyond that a major highway. You'll figure out the rest. Here—turn here!"

Sharon pulled in to a short lane, and the professor jumped out of the car to run up to a wooden cottage peeking through the trees. When Sharon and Tatyana came in behind him, he had a small trowel in his hand and was pushing a table across the floor. Packages of buckwheat and flour fell to the floor, canned food rolling into the corners of the small, one room cottage. Sharon and Tatyana quickly rushed to help him.

"They're buried here, under this table," he said breathlessly. He slammed the point of the trowel into the packed dirt floor, and frantically began to dig. A moment later he was pulling a plastic shopping bag from the ground.

The door crashed opened, startling Tatyana and the professor. A man stood in the doorway. The gun in his hands was leveled at Sharon. A second later, two more gun-toting men rushed in behind him.

The first man paused for a split second, ever so subtly reacting to their entrance.

The tiny distraction was all Sharon needed. Like lightning, she twisted the gun out of the first man's hand, unleashed two shots into his chest, and sent another three rounds into the FSB officer by the door. She assertively moved towards the last man, letting Tatyana and the professor escape, and pulled the trigger. Nothing; the gun was jammed. Without skipping a beat, Sharon maneuvered around the officer and with serpentine precision struck the gun out of his hand and landed a blow to the back of his neck.

The FSB officer swiftly pulled his knife out and lunged at Sharon. A miss. He tried again. Another miss. He had never before encountered such a professional and began to more carefully close in on her.

Sharon calmly pressed herself against the table. She realized that he was trying to force her into a corner. She moved her right hand behind her back and grabbed one of the remaining bags of flour. Before the officer could strike again, she launched the bag of flour at him and landed a solid kick to the man's chest. Blood burst from the man mouth. Sharon watched, confused, as he fell to his knees. Then she saw Tatyana standing behind him, a pitchfork jammed into his back. She let go of the handle, and the man fell face first next to Sharon. Sharon stepped over him, lightly hugged Tatyana, and whispered, "Thank you."

They heard a motor running outside. The two women stepped through the door just as the professor pulled up to them. He scurried out of the driver's seat and jumped into the back seat, saying, "C'mon, quick getaway!"

Sharon slid behind the wheel, and pressed the pedal to the floor. They screamed away from the cottage, and were almost to the end of the lane when a car pulled in, blocking their way. Sharon slammed on the brakes, and the car fishtailed for a moment before grinding to a halt.

Tatyana groaned loudly, sinking down into her seat. Without taking her eyes off the car, Sharon tossed a lighter into the backseat.

"If it goes bad, you know what to do professor." The only response was a whimper.

Suddenly the car's lights flickered in a familiar patterns, and Sharon breathed a sigh of relief. "Relax, they're with us."

"Are you sure?" Tatyana hissed.

Sharon opened her car door. The passenger side of the other car opened as well, and a non-descript man stepped out. Before getting out of the car, Sharon asked for the professor's blazer and the tracker. "If anyone ever asks, someone stole your blazer, okay, professor?" She stepped out and handed it to the man from the other car. "Disinfect everything. No trace left behind. Throw the blazer somewhere in the village five kilometers up the road."

The man nodded once and headed back to the car.

"And I need an extra set of hands to help the professor," Sharon called out. She stuck her head back into the car. "We'll scan the documents and leave the originals with you. We are not ready to take them with us."

The two cars returned to the cottage, where the newcomers made themselves busy. Tatyana watched in a daze as they removed the bodies, swept up the flour, and filled in the hole in the ground. The Russians would know what happened here, but they carefully wiped away all traceable prints, bullets, and blood stains. Sharon and the professor stood off to the side, scanning the documents with Sharon's "mirror". Within fifteen minutes, the cottage was back to its original condition. The marks where bullets had ricocheted in the room now looked, at first glance, like unremarkable wear-and-tear in an old cottage.

The professor pulled Sharon to one side as the crew walked towards the cars. "This is the formula for the poison intended for the rulers of Western Europe, and your president," he said, opening a folder. "I will develop this antidote first. But remember, they always have a plan B."

Tatyana felt like she didn't catch her breath until she was through airport security and settled into her small plane seat. After twenty minutes of silence, Sharon leaned close to her. "I am amazed by you, you know. You turned out to be a reliable partner, ready to sacrifice yourself."

Tatyana laughed nervously. "Oh, I don't know about that. I was lost at first. I'm just a simple journalist. But I guess my survival instincts kicked in there at the end."

"And just in time."

Tatyana turned to face her. "You know what I can't stop thinking about?"

"What?"

"We have this one deputy in the Ukrainian parliament who talks about putting all of Putin's freaks on a pitchfork. A pitchfork is probably standing next to the Ukrainian flag in his office." She grinned devilishly and held up a finger. "One down."

Sharon smiled.

"Now if we could just dismantle Putin's propaganda machine, we'll have won the war. Easy, right?"

This time, Sharon snorted.

They were silent for several moments before Tatyana spoke again.

"It wouldn't be that hard, actually."

"What, dismantling the propaganda machine?"

Tatyana nodded.

"And just how do you propose to do what world leaders haven't been able to do?"

"With the right understanding of the audience's interests and the right collection of programs, we could neutralize or even destroy the influence of Putin's propaganda machine. Not just in Russia, but in all regions of the world."

"Ah, but only if we didn't have this dirty little word...*bureaucracy.*"

Tatyana leaned back in her seat and closed her eyes. "Don't worry about that. I've got a whole battalion of journalists who despise the word. We'll take the enemy down."

Sharon looked at her with admiration. She had no doubts that Tatyana would do exactly that.

CHAPTER 14

Alexander stood at the CIA building in Virginia, staring at the nameless stars on the marble wall. Next to the wall was a book protected under glass. The glass was inlaid with three red roses. In the book, in calligraphic handwriting, were written the names of several men and women who had died in the line of duty. Alexander stretched his arm alongside the wall, as if saluting the fallen.

Sharon walked up behind him and quietly waited for him.

"Thanks to the living and the fallen," Alexander whispered, turning to Sharon. "Sharon, if something happens to me, will my star be here as well?"

"Well first of all, nothing will happen to you," Sharon answered briskly. "And, second, your star won't be here. It'll be waiting for you in Kiev, in St. Sophia's Cathedral in a white dress. Just don't forget to invite us to the wedding."

As she led him to the office she asked, "Are you free tonight? Tom and I would like to host you for dinner."

Alexander shrugged. "No plans. Will 6:30 work?"

"Perfect." She gave him a quick tour of the public areas and stopped for some coffee in the cafeteria. By 11:00, they were seated in a small, simple office. Unlike the GRU offices in Moscow, there weren't any expensive, fancy tables or posh chairs.

A tall, lean man with close-cropped hair walked in and closed the door. "Ed Johnson," he said, holding out a hand to Alexander. "I'm responsible for your operation on this side of the Atlantic. Heard a lot about you."

Alexander chuckled. "All good I hope?"

Ed smiled. "Nothing bad." He motioned toward a chair. "Take a seat right here. I'm excited about what you've already done and what you're doing now. As you know, Putin has already offered the Seven an important meeting in Brussels. Our leaders have agreed, without knowing what stands behind it. Help me to understand, Alexander, why he has decided to take such risk, to poison all of them?"

"Because you have cornered him with your sanctions and ridiculed him on an international stage. He has nothing to lose. He wants payback all at once. He wants to finish your leaders before his own people realize their mistake."

"We will need to develop a detailed plan of the operation to arrest Mr. Putin, code name Scorpion." He checked his notes in a file, then looked up at Alexander. "What's the situation with the rug? Need any help?"

Alexander shook his head. "I spoke with General Malinkov yesterday. The rug's in Brussels already and is officially registered as property of the Russian Federation." Alexander pulled a photo from his jacket pocket and handed it to Ed.

The picture showed a tapestry of white, blue and red with a two-headed eagle in the center—the symbol of Russia.

"Beautiful," Ed said. "And quite impressive. This will give you and Sharon a lot more room to maneuver on the territory of the Russian Federation, so to speak, in case of unforeseen situations." He stood and opened the door. "Let's move to our video room, I want to show you the analysis we've put together on Putin. All of his movements and steps have been calculated to the second." He pointed them down the hall. "Second door on the left."

Once inside, Alexander closed the door behind them and took a seat. Ed dimmed the lights, and flicked on a projector. With the videos queued up, the plan unfolded.

"As you can see," Ed continued, "they show you exactly where General Malinkov's men will have to be in order to quietly neutralize Putin's bodyguard. Sharon will offer her hand to him, and you will come in for the arrest. Keep in mind he must be arrested only while standing on that rug. By international law, that rug is considered Russian property and territory, so you only have the authority as a Russian official to take him then. As soon you do, you will hand him over to our Special Forces. We cannot violate international law regarding presidential immunity."

Ed turned off the video and flipped on the lights. "Any questions?"

There were none, and at 6:30, Alexander was standing at the door of Tom and Sharon's home. An unfamiliar, elderly man opened the door, and an elegant woman peered out from behind him.

"You must be Alexander," she said, pushing past the man to hold out her hand to Alexander. An impressively-sized diamond decorated her manicured hands.

Alexander shook her hand and nodded.

"I'm Sarah, and this is my husband Joseph."

"If you give me the chance, I could welcome our guest as well," Joseph said gruffly.

"It's not my fault that you always do everything too late, Joseph," Sarah muttered to him. Raising her voice slightly, she continued, "Of course, of course, Joseph please meet our guest Alexander. But why are we standing in the doorway? Come in, Alexander. Dear, move over and let him pass," she commanded restlessly.

As she clicked away in her heels, Joseph shrugged good-naturedly. "Don't pay her any attention," he said, loudly enough for Sarah to hear. "She's heard a lot of good things about you and is a bit star-struck. Wouldn't even allow Tom or Sharon to answer their own door!"

"I'm grateful for such attention," Alexander said, a bit awkwardly. He took a few steps into the house and glanced around, taking in small details.

Tom and Sharon walked into the hallway at that moment. "Everyone acquainted?" Tom asked cheerfully.

Alexander laughed. "We're in the process still."

Sharon pushed past the others to link arms with Alexander. "Give him some room, please. Lots more people to meet." She led Alexander down the hallway and turned him into the living room, where another ten people waited. As soon as he entered the room, Alexander got the distinct impression that, while he didn't know or recognize anyone, they all knew him. Much like Tom and Sharon, though, they were easy to make friends with. It was a matter of minutes before Alexander starting feeling welcome, amid the cheerful bubble of conversation and smiles. It was like they had known each other for years, in no time at all.

At five minutes to 7:00, Sharon invited all the guests to the table. Alexander was surprised to see that there were name cards at each place, like at a wedding. He found his own, and along with everyone else took a seat in the designated spot. He was placed in the center. He suspected something unusual was taking place.

Tom stood, picked up a glass of wine in his right hand, and a remote control in his left. "Dear friends, I am incredibly thankful that you are always ready to help, when help is needed and when it is difficult. Before we discuss anything, I want to make this toast to Alexander and his love, Tatyana."

Alexander was bewildered at first. He had only begun to process what had been said when, suddenly, the huge clock in the corner of the living room chimed, as if perfectly timed for Tom's speech. Tom clicked the remote, and the large TV screen flickered on. Everyone turned toward the television.

An all-too-familiar voice began to speak in Russian. Alexander realized immediately that it was Tatyana, opening the first broadcast of Euro-American television. She was presenting each of the countries in the European Union, NATO, and their allies, introducing the viewers to the television and radio broadcasting programs.

"Today, the media has become a boundless battlefield—an information war for the minds and hearts of the people. The Euro-American television program will help all of us get to know each other better, and understand each other more completely, so that we can prevent dictatorial reigns like that of Putin from taking hold. Make no mistake, the Russian propaganda machine is powerful, and Putin has used it to strengthen his foothold in the world. We believe that this, the first day of airing the Euro-American television and radio broadcast, will be the last day of Putin's vile and deceitful propaganda." The English subtitles could barely keep up with Tatyana's words as she spoke them.

As she finished this last sentence, the other dinner guests began to applaud and cheer, "bravo," and "salud," drowning out Tatyana's voice.

"To your health!" Tony shouted in Russian, before emptying his glass. Everyone followed his example. Then everything was quiet again. All eyes remained fixed on the TV.

Tatyana's voice took on a fiercer tone. "And to our compatriots, wherever you may be, you will be able to tune into the Euro-American international broadcasting program 'Kievan Rus.' At the conclusion of our program, we will be sharing some news that will not be very pleasant for the Russian Federation. With each passing day, the struggle of Kuban, Siberia, the Urals, Königsberg, and other regions seeking to leave the Russian Federation is becoming more and more apparent. On the streets of the Far East, we are increasingly seeing posters and rallies calling for the creation of the Far East People's Republic. Demonstrations are taking place in the streets of the Urals and Siberia. Siberians are marching through their cities with their own flag! None of these regions wants to feed the Kremlin magnates anymore.

"Make no mistake. Civil war is brewing. Putin's solution to citizens' hunger and cold is to let them die. The dead do not go hungry. The dead don't freeze. Leading scientists are fleeing the country. Those left behind melt into the chaos and corruption of Russia. As for Putin, he has already proven himself in the eyes of the civilized world and history as a man with the mentality of primitive society, capable of only using natural resources—namely, natural gas and oil. Mongol-Tatar blood is boiling in his veins.

He cannot come to terms with the fact that soon he will not have anyone from which to collect tribute."

After the last words, a flurry of applause once again filled the room. Alexander was showered with compliments and congratulations, as if he had been the one hosting this broadcast. He felt uncomfortable to some extent; it was strange seeing—or rather, hearing—Tatyana in such an official, exposed capacity. And as much as he enjoyed his new friends, it felt strange for them to be so vocal in their support of a woman that, for all he knew, none of them had ever met.

This time it was Sharon who stood, holding a glass of wine with both hands. The others around the table quieted, and turned toward her. She spoke quietly, but everyone listened without making a noise.

"Not long ago, Tatyana and I flew together from Siberia. She shared with me her dream of a broadcast program like this." She smiled. "Today, her dream came true. And Alexander, please forgive us for the secrecy. Tatyana really wanted this moment to be a surprise for you. And just one last surprise: all the guests here tonight are her sponsors—whom clearly she did not disappoint!"

Alexander smiled, stood up halfway from the table, put his hand over his heart, and respectfully nodded several times. "Thank you, ladies and gentlemen, thank all of you. All of this has surpassed my expectations," he said in an emotional voice. He straightened, took a glass in his hand, and said, "Sharon, if you don't mind, would you allow me to give this toast?"

"It's not polite to interrupt women," Sharon said playfully, "but today we will make an exception for you." She raised the glass in her left hand.

"To the beautiful Sharon, and to each of you, my dear friends," Alexander said enthusiastically.

Again the bells of the crystal glasses rang. The diamond on Sarah's finger flashed like lightning, and the room was filled with thunderous applause.

After drinking, Sharon winked at Alexander. "Thank you, Alexander. But as I have made an exception for you, I hope you will do me the same honor and answer a simple question."

"If as an exception, then yes, you can." Alexander said jokingly.

"Tell us honestly, dear, did you already propose to your love?"

Not for the first time that evening, Alexander was taken aback. He would never get used to the forwardness of Americans! "Well we haven't seen each other for quite a while, she being on one end of America and I on the other," was all he could muster.

Sharon cut off his boyish excuses, to the delight of the rest of the guests. "Answer the question: Have you proposed to her? Yes or no?"

He hung his head. There was no avoiding it. "No, I haven't," he answered.

"My dear," Sarah interrupted, "Take my experience to heart and try to not procrastinate with this. Those like her do not go unnoticed here, and I don't want to see someone get ahead of you."

"I promise you I will pop the question in the near future." He abruptly pulled the tie from his neck and unbuttoned the collar of his shirt. He removed a gold chain from within his shirt. At the end of it flashed a white gold ring decorated with a small, modest-sized diamond. "Wherever I am, alive or dead, she is always with me. At the first opportunity I get, I will gladly put this ring on her finger."

Sarah squinted, exaggeratedly trying to get a better look at the ring. "I'm glad that gentlemen are not yet extinct on this planet," she said, satisfied. "Joseph also gifted me with a ring, except he did not wear it around his neck close to his heart day and night.

He kept it in a desk somewhere, right. Joseph? Confess in front of all of us."

Joseph leaned over and kissed Sarah's cheek. "Does it really matter where I kept it?" He held up her hand for all to see. "More importantly, look at how this diamond has grown!"

There were chuckles all around the table.

"Point taken," Alexander said. "I'll 'feed' this diamond as well."

The ceremony over, the guests turned to their own conversations. Dinner was brought out, and everyone began to eat spiritedly. They were clearly enjoying the evening, with the scent of revolution and love in the air. Alexander picked at his food for a while, then quietly excused himself. He quietly went to the second floor, where he found a guest room and closed the door behind him for some privacy. He took out his phone and slowly dialed.

A man's voice answered. "Yes?"

"Father Michael, it's me, Alexander."

"What a joy to hear your voice! How can I help you?"

Alexander hesitated. Considering what he and the priest had been through, his request was no doubt going to come as a surprise. "Well, I plan to marry Tatyana, but she's religious and has been baptized, while I have not."

Silence on the other end. "Do you believe in God?" Michael asked solemnly after what seemed like an eternity.

Alexander sat down on the guest bed, and ran his fingers through his hair. "I don't even know. It seems like I have felt his hands guiding my life, but can I call myself a believer? I just don't know."

"Let's approach it from a different angle," Father Michael answered. "Would you call yourself an atheist?"

"Absolutely not," Alexander answered immediately.

Michael chuckled on the other end. "So when you get the chance, come for a visit and we will baptize you in the Jordan River."

"In Israel?" Alexander asked, deeply confused.

Again, Michael laughed, louder this time. "We have our own Jordan, Alexander. You just might know it as the Dnepr."

Alexander said nothing, still confused. Father Michael sensed this and explained.

"In the history of all mankind, the mass baptism of nations took place in only two rivers: the Jordan River during the days of Christ, and the Dnepr River in 988, during the reign of Prince Vladimir Svyatoslavich. Since that time we have come to know the Dnepr as our holy river."

"Alright," Alexander said as he swallowed the lump that had suddenly appeared in his throat, "baptism in our Jordan will do just fine."

"Very good," Michael replied. "Is there anything else?"

"Actually, yes. I know that Tatyana dreams of getting married in St. Sophia's Cathedral. What is needed for this? Will you be able to officiate our wedding there?"

"Have you at least proposed to her yet?"

Alexander rolled his eyes. "You are all conspiring against me, huh? I am calling her as soon as I finish with you."

"Don't worry Alexander, we will try to make her dream become reality."

Alexander thanked the warrior-turned-priest, and hung up. Before he could dial Tatyana's phone number, however, a soft knock sounded on the door.

"I'm not disturbing you, am I?" Sharon asked, peering into the room as she opened the door a crack.

Alexander shook his head. "Just following orders and making arrangements for the wedding location." He stood up and pocketed his phone.

She clapped lightly. "I knew you had it in you!" She stepped through the door and lowered her voice. "The Center just called. We fly out tonight, at 3:00 AM. Looks like our celebration banquet has come to an end. General Malinkov is already in Brussels. He appointed you to be in charge from the Russian side. On our side, Ed remains in charge."

"Me?" Alexander was shocked. He had expected this.

"The General said he must be in Russia. The country is on the brink of a civil war. Putin may resort to military force at any moment. If the army generals refuse to carry out his orders, he will send the National Guard. The General said that it is difficult to predict how the country will react when Putin is arrested. He doesn't want to take any additional risks."

Alexander nodded and followed Sharon from the room. He made his way to the dining room, to say his goodbyes, only to find that all the guests had left already. Even Tom had unexpectedly left, apparently with someone from the Pentagon. He thanked Sharon for the party and raced home to pack.

The yellow taxi pulled up to the international terminal of the Dulles airport and stopped near the Lufthansa airline section. Alexander paid the taxi driver in no hurry, took his small sports bag from the back seat, opened the door, and again in no hurry, headed towards the huge glass doors of the terminal. Despite the late hour, there were still many people at the airport.

His cell phone rang. Alexander looked at the number. "Yes, Sharon?"

"Don't pass me by. Look left." Sharon sat at a small table in Starbucks, waving to him.

Alexander joined her. "Did you speak to Tom before leaving?" he said as he sat down.

Sharon frowned. "No. Couldn't get a hold of him. I left a few messages on his cell phone. I even wrote him a small letter, like we did in our younger days. Expressed my love to him and apologized if there was anything wrong on my part."

"How often do you guys have these explanations?"

Sharon looked down at her coffee. "When we worked in Russia, quite often. We didn't write much. Just a few heartwarming lines. We were fulfilling our tasks, which meant no guarantees of a return." She sighed heavily as she remembered. "Sometimes we would go without seeing each other for months. Those few warm lines were a lifesaver."

Alexander pulled out his cell phone.

"What are you doing?"

He smiled. "Following your example. Sending Tatyana a couple of heartwarming lines. After all, I too haven't seen her for several months now, and a lot of unexpected things can happen on this mission."

"You might see her sooner than you think," Sharon said, a bit smugly.

Alexander shot her a glance. "What do you mean?"

"Her team is recording Putin's arrest."

Alexander stared at her with incredulity. "Does she know that?"

A mischievous smile played across Sharon's lips. "She only knows what a journalist should know: something unusual, interesting, and important is happening. And her group has been cut off from the outside world. No cell phones. No internet."

"Where is she now?"

"Don't know for sure." Sharon watched Alexander over the top of her coffee cup. "Don't be upset that she didn't call you. This was all a surprise to her as well."

He shrugged. "Not upset. Work is work." He fidgeted with his own coffee cup. "When will she find out about everything?"

"A few minutes before the operation. Just enough time to accept what is happening so they don't freeze up from shock when things get going."

A man and woman approached their table, each carrying attaché cases. They had the universal look of intelligence personnel. Sharon stood, her face lighting up with recognition. "I can't believe my eyes," she said. She hugged each of them in turn. "How many years, Ben? How many winters, Alice?"

"It's been some time," Ben said, adjusting his thick glasses. "But now is not the time for catching up." They placed the leather attaché cases on the floor. "Everything you need from the laboratory. Including instructions. Bulletproof cases, and they do not burn. The locks are coded. You'll get the codes in a text message." He cleared his throat, and Alice glanced around the coffee shop. Just as quickly as they appeared, the pair was gone.

Alexander and Sharon finished their drinks and made their way toward the plane. Although a few of the seats were already occupied, they were only concerned with the military man leaning against a window in the middle of the plane, a cap tightly pulled over his eyes. The insignia on his shoulders identified him as a NATO pilot. He was snoring lightly. Alexander and Sharon exchanged wary glances. He was seated right behind them. They took their seats carefully, trying not to wake him.

As the plane engine started up, Sharon pulled out her phone and checked for messages. There were none. "I'm going to try calling Tom once more."

"Not afraid to wake our neighbor?" Alexander glanced over his shoulder.

"I'll be quiet. If he answers, I'll move to the other end of the plane." Sharon chewed on her lip for a moment, staring at the phone. Finally she dialed his number. The phone rang a few times. She was about to hang up when Tom's quiet voice answered. "Finally!" she exclaimed in relief.

Sharon rose from her seat and quickly went to the nose of the plane, holding the phone to her ear. "Where are you? What happened? How come I couldn't reach you?"

"Don't worry dear, I am always with you."

"Listen, I made your favorite soup. It's in the refrigerator. Don't forget to feed Kevin. He's been asking me to make this soup for a while now."

"Thank you, darling. It's a very delicious soup. Very delicious."

Alexander was watching Sharon speak into the phone when he heard movement behind him. He glanced back over his shoulder, then stood in disbelief, staring at his neighbor.

Tom, his cap now raised, held a finger to his lips, signaling to Alexander to be silent, as he spoke into the phone. Before Alexander could return to his seat, Sharon looked back briefly. There was a brief confusion, followed quickly by surprise. Surprise gave way to anger as she recognized him and quickly marched back to her seat.

Tom didn't have time to react as the formidable Sharon stared down at him.

"Now wait a minute, honey," Tom said, scrambling to his feet, holding out is hands in a placating manner. "Let me explain. People will be boarding soon and you don't want to make a scene."

Sharon crossed her arms and gave him a withering look.

"Now, honey, you can't give me the silent treatment the whole trip. It didn't work in Istanbul, right?"

Her eyes narrowed. "Watch me!" She turned her back on him and collapsed into the chair in front of him with a loud "harrumph!"

Tom stood and moved to the same row, sitting in the seat next to her.

"Just what do you think you're doing?" Sharon demanded.

"Taking my seat. Here's my ticket, look."

Sharon looked at the ticket reluctantly. After a few minutes, her shoulders relaxed a little. Tom took this as his cue to try to explain. He leaned over to whisper in her ear.

"I'm sorry, Sharon, but I gave Russia twenty years of my life—most of them directly to Putin. I could not miss such a significant moment. It took some finagling, but I finally got appointed as your chaperone."

"Is that what you are doing in this crazy uniform?" Sharon asked, all the anger gone from her voice.

"I think I look rather spiffy."

Sharon half-snorted, half-laughed. "If actual NATO pilots looked like you, none of us would feel safe flying."

"Oh, come on," Tom said, a small smile finally making its way to his face. "You're happy I'm here."

Sharon hated to admit it, but he was right. Alexander, who hadn't felt this tense since Donetsk, relaxed, and soon the three of them were asleep.

The days moved slowly, despite being filled with information and training exercises, repeated viewings of videos, calculations and recalculations. Alexander and Sharon ran through the plan with one another constantly. On the third day, the monotony was broken when Ed called Sharon and Alexander into his office to inform them that Putin's Special Forces had picked up Professor Mosin and taken him to the airport.

"In handcuffs?" Alexander asked.

Ed shook his head. "No handcuffs, no belongings."

Sharon nodded. "With Professor Mosin, Putin has both a hostage and a skilled chemist knowledgeable about poisons and antidotes."

"They won't leave such a valuable resource unprotected," Alexander said. "If something goes wrong, they won't leave him alive. No witnesses."

Ed heaved a deep sigh. "I'm meeting with General Malinkov in two hours. Maybe he'll have a solution."

Sharon and Alexander started to leave, but Ed stopped them.

"The laboratory has tested the poison and antidotes, but we need a practical experiment today so we know how long the litmus ointment is visible–"

"Two seconds," Sharon interrupted. "We checked for ourselves."

That had *not* been Alexander's idea. He was getting as bored as anyone else stuck in one place waiting for something momentous to happen. But Sharon was something else entirely. She had come up with a plan to sneak into the small lab attached to the CIA office, and pressure the chemist there to test the litmus ointment on them. There was no way to get a proper reading without actually using the poison, so the day before, Alexander had suddenly found himself sitting next to Sharon, as a reluctant and petrified Russian chemist dabbed their forearms with Putin's poison. She grinned the whole time.

Ed stared at her in disbelief. "Are you *crazy?*"

"Maybe so," Sharon said, shrugging. "But we're still alive."

Putin's Il-96 aircraft arrived right on time at 7:30 in the evening, touching down on the Brussels' runway and taxiing to the assigned parking spot. Six black Mercedes accompanied it. Three other cars carrying Russian Embassy officials approached the plane. Russian media was already set up to record the arrival. The bright lights lining the runway glinted off their numerous cameras.

At the last minute, the president's plane taxied to a new spot on the other side of the airport. Soon, the plane completely disappeared behind the airport building. The media representatives stumbled over themselves trying to follow. Suddenly, a large, luxurious bus appeared and rolled to a stop. A pretty woman stepped out. In broken Russian, she apologized for the change in locations. For security reasons, the Russian president's plane would be parked in lot number thirty—an area requiring a special vehicle permit for entrance. It was a lengthy approval process, she noted. The airport administration had sent the bus to take them to the correct area in comfort.

The journalists grabbed their equipment and dragged it to the bus. Embassy representatives moved more slowly, grumbling as they waited to board. A few tried to use their phones, but they found no reception. Finally, filled to the brim, the bus quietly left for the other area, stopping only once to drop off the pretty brunette.

The bus driver continued around the airport.

"Where are we going?" one of the Embassy staff asked.

"Special route. Buses only," the driver called back.

"Just pick up the pace," the staff member said. "We're already late."

As if on cue, a police car pulled in front of the bus and signaled for the driver to pull over.

"Great," the driver mumbled. "Now I'm getting a ticket for speeding."

Moments later, several police officers boarded the bus and asked to see everyone's documents.

"Putin will never forgive us for this," the Russian ambassador whispered quietly.

Meanwhile, on the tarmac, the Russian aircraft sat still, far to the side of the airport's central building. A small group of journalists with TV cameras was already waiting. As soon as the plane stopped, the pilot turned off the engine, steps were driven to the door, and a passenger truck neared. Four strong-looking guys jumped out of it and unfurled a huge rug in front of the steps. When finished, the truck drove off.

The limited light highlighted the bluish-white background of the Russian double-headed eagle trimmed in gold. The six Mercedes accompanying the plane stopped in a tight semicircle, just steps from the corner of the rug, leaving a little more space on the left side. They effectively completely blocked surveillance from the airport side.

The car doors opened, and civilians and military men alike exited. Some stood on the rug; others positioned themselves around it. All of them were talking among themselves about something, smiling and laughing. Two cameras from different angles were directed at the door of the aircraft; two more covered the greeters from different angles. A reporter was speaking into a microphone, glancing at the door of the aircraft every so often.

All were ready for the arrival of the great guest.

When the door of the aircraft finally opened, one of the pilots appeared on the steps, followed by another one in civilian clothing. They affixed the stairs to the fuselage. Then a woman appeared on the gangway, standing along the right-hand side. The wind gently fluttered her blonde hair. She occasionally looked inside the cabin. After a few minutes, more people appeared at the door.

A large black limousine sporting Russian flags and the emblem of the Russian Federation approached the aircraft and stopped in the area reserved for it, to the left side of the rug. Its mirrors reflected the light of the projectors. One of the TV cameras turned toward the limousine. The others remained focused on the aircraft doors and the greeters.

President Putin emerged and stood at the top of the step. The greeters applauded. The president smiled softly, with some restraint. His face was set hard. He raised his right hand to wave to everyone. He started down the stairs, a slight limp in his right leg.

The driver of the Mercedes parked opposite the steps got out and opened the rear door of the car. Sharon emerged, sporting an elegant hairstyle, a red blazer with crisp black outlines over a white blouse and pencil skirt, a pearl necklace, and high heels that made her simply irresistible. Her slim gait emphasized her fit body. In measured stride, she walked to meet Putin. The sharp *click* of her hears gave way to the sound of muffled steps as she walked across the carpet.

Putin couldn't take his eyes off her. Sharon noticed.

She calculated the steps she would need to reach Putin in the middle of the rug. She and Alexander had practiced this in the CIA office. They had shoved the furniture aside and marked off the area of the rug with tape. Despite the practice, there was still no telling how quickly or slowly Putin would approach.

As the president moved towards Sharon, he seemed to stand a little taller, his limping lessened. Camera bulbs flashed like lightening, and all eyes were on them. Just a few steps separated them from the middle of the rug.

Finally, they both set foot on the chest of the Russian double-headed eagle at the same time: Putin on one side, Sharon on the other. They were even an arm's length apart. They stopped and watched each other. Putin wore thin gloves. They weren't meant to keep the fingers warm; they were to protect him from contact with others. Sharon quickly noted that none of those accompanying Putin were wearing gloves. She saw Putin hesitate, trying to decide whether to offer his hand or not, take the glove off or not.

Sharon took the initiative. "Vladimir Vladimirovich, I am pleased to welcome you." She held out her hand to him with a charming smile.

He hesitated for the tiniest of seconds. "I am pleased to meet you as well." He didn't look her in the eye.

Sharon kept her smile firmly in place and spoke through her teeth so that only Putin heard her words. "Vladimir Vladimirovich, would you not deign to shake a lady's hand with so many cameras watching us? A proud knight with mighty powers wouldn't embarrass her like that publicly in front of millions of TV viewers, especially when she was sent as a representative of the White House."

Putin brightened up immediately and stripped off a glove. "Of course, I am honored to shake the hand of one as lovely as yourself."

Still, he was not looking her in the eye. With half-parted lips, he was looking down at their hands.

"Vladimir Vladimirovich, I sincerely hope that the relations between our countries, between Russia and the Western world, will continue to improve, that we can become friends." Sharon was in no hurry to let go of Putin's hand. A purple hue appeared on her skin, and she covered her right hand with her left one.

"We will take all possible measures to ensure that our relations improve," Putin said hurriedly. He was no longer looking at Sharon.

"I am grateful for such warm hope." She nearly imperceptibly nodded her head twice. It was the signal the others had been waiting for. The poison on her hands, the litmus ointment, had worked.

It was not apparent that he knew what was taking place, but he had become tight-lipped and nervous. Putin practically tore his grip from Sharon's and hastily put on his glove. Sharon stood unmoving, smiling professionally. Putin frowned slightly.

"May I pass?"

"Of course, Vladimir Vladimirovich. This is your limousine." She nodded to the left, gesturing with hand, palm down. A tall, middle-aged, broad-shouldered man stood by the car, dressed smartly in a two-piece charcoal suit.

Before Putin could move forward, the tall man opened the back door of the limousine. Alexander stepped out, dressed in a black jacket, white shirt, and navy tie with the Russian coat of arms and a gold clip. On the left side of the jacket was a small icon: the Russian Federation flag. He took two steps and stood directly in front of Putin.

Putin took a step forward, expecting Alexander to move aside. Instead, Alexander held up a hand. Putin did not reciprocate. Alexander's hand hung in the air. Putin studied Alexander from head to toe. He tried to take another step forward, but Alexander's palm landed flatly against Putin's chest.

"Are you Vladimir Vladimirovich Putin?" Alexander asked without taking his hand off Putin's chest.

Fury blazed in the dictator's eyes. "Remove your hand immediately or I will remove it for you."

"I am Alexander Denisovich Ivanov, of the Federal Security Service. According to the Criminal Code of the Russian Federation and International Law, you, citizen Putin, are arrested and charged with crimes against humanity."

The circle around Putin tightened, leaving a small space for two TV cameras. Alexander was dimly aware of Tatyana's voice, off to his left. She was providing a running commentary, describing the events as they unfolded. Several men who had disembarked after Putin placed hands on the breasts of their suits, feeling for their sidearms. They glanced at one another, unsure of what to do. They began to realize that there were significantly fewer of them than had been planned.

Two generals stepped forward, each taking hold of one of Putin's elbows. "Don't try anything stupid," one of them said.

Putin was franticly searching for his bodyguards, who still milled about the periphery of the rug.

"With the exception of those clowns, they're all neutralized," the other general said. "Alive, but fast asleep," he corrected himself.

"Is this some kind of stupid prank?" Putin blurted out.

"Not as stupid as your pranks in Crimea and Eastern Ukraine—and in your gloves here today," Alexander said loudly and sternly.

Putin tried to jerk free, but suddenly his arms were behind him and the second general snapped handcuffs into place. The generals brought him to the edge of the rug. Putin still had some strength in him, and despite his limp he tensed his body and resisted, forcing the generals to plant their feet and push him forward.

"Citizen Putin," Alexander continued with the same stern voice. "From this moment you are being transferred into the hands of international justice. You have the right to remain silent."

Putin did not hear the words. The back door of the car opened once again. Tom stepped out, and Putin studied him carefully, as if trying to remembering something.

"Yes, we've met a few times in the Kremlin," Tom said quietly. "You signed this verdict yourself. We stood with you to raise a toast to the new Russia. Too bad you did not meet the expectations of your people or of the international community. You didn't lead Russia where it should have gone." Tom held open the rear door of the limousine.

Putin glared at Tom. With a restrained, metallic voice, he said, "I have to wash my hands."

"From the blood or the poison?" Tom asked coldly.

Silently and with a flattened lip, Putin continued to stare at Tom.

"It's not pleasant to die from your own invention, is it? Try to step into the shoes of those to whom you weren't so humane." Tom let his words sink in. "The antidote will continue to work for six more hours. Let's hope Professor Mosin remains safe so you don't die before the international tribunal."

"Where is he?" Putin gasped, already getting into the car.

"Alive and well. You will meet with him soon, but at the right time and in the right place."

Two strong men joined Putin on either side. Tom closed the limousine door. The Cadillac sped away. Tom, Sharon, and Alexander, as if for the first time, heard the questions being yelled by reporters. They seemed to be accosting anyone wearing a uniform.

"What's going on? Has the president truly been arrested? Sir, please explain; what poison?" NATO soldiers had their work cut out for them as the media and their cameras pushed forward. Never once did the cameras stop flashing. One journalist, however, was let through.

Tom found Sharon and hugged her tightly. Tatyana cleared her throat to interrupt them, a microphone in her hand. Alexander had never seen her as beautiful as she was just then. "Care to explain what just happened for our viewers?" she asked smartly, her excitement and pride evident from the smile across her lips.

"With great pleasure," Sharon said. "But I will say, this handsome man was the true hero of the evening."

She reached out for Alexander, and all the camera lights swiveled to him. He squinted and smiled sheepishly. Tatyana stepped forward, her cheeks flushed bright red. "Congratulations on a successful mission," she said in a breathy voice.

"Thank you," Alexander said before bending down closer to the microphone. "But I have one more task to complete tonight."

All eyes turned to Alexander, who pulled the chain from around his neck. He bent to one knee, jerked the chain from his neck, and then opened his fist to reveal the ring. "Tatyana, help me complete my mission and marry me. Will you be my wife?"

Liquid pearls rolled down her cheeks from his words. Her professional demeanor slipped, and she said, "Of course!" Never one to miss a soundbite, though, she held onto the microphone in her left hand, and wiped away a tear while hugging Alexander with her right. He awkwardly slid the ring on her finger.

This was too much for the photographers. What had promised to be an interesting photo-op had turned into an unprecedented whirlwind of events, and they could barely keep up. The light October breeze carried the thunderous applause and joyful shouts of "bravo!" into the night. Sharon and Tom came up to Tatyana and Alexander.

"So you've just pulled off the event of the century. Where are we off to now?" Tom asked.

Before Alexander could answer, Ed approached him. In his extended hand was a phone. "What is this?"

"General Malinkov," Ed replied.

"Did something happen?" Alexander asked with mounting tension in his voice.

"He will tell you."

The End

About the Author

Val Taube was born and raised in the former Soviet Union, where he also graduated from university. His professional experience as a historian has enabled him to develop a deep understanding of the KGB's work.

He also draws from a well of personal experience, as his family has been politically active for generations. With *Divided Empire,* Val hopes readers can learn to identify and analyze the indicators of harmful propaganda in modern-day news sources.